Close-Ups

Winner of

Close-Ups

Stories by Sandra Thompson

The University of Georgia Press
Athens

2/1984
gen'l

Library of Congress Cataloging in Publication Data

Thompson, Sandra.
    Close-ups : stories.

    I. Title.
PS3570.H6436C4 1984   813'.54   83-4981
ISBN 0-8203-0683-5

For my daughter,
ALEXANDRA

. . . the summer is ended, and we are not saved.

—Jeremiah 8:20

Contents

One

Horror Show

My brother, soft palms and knees moving silently across the carpet, approaches me lying above him on the bed, unsuspecting. It is his favorite game, "Ribs." He is the character Ribs, and I am me. He raises himself to the height of the bed, rests his chin on it, level with my body, and as he makes his ascent up the side of the bed, the trip from the foot of the bed to where I am lying near the pillows, he mutters, "I am going to kill you." At five his enunciation is crisp and he knows how to raise his voice on "kill" and drag that word out slowly, through his teeth. Ten years later, the walls of his room are covered with posters: of the Wolf Man, Dracula, the Frankenstein monster, whom he affectionately calls Frankie. The Thing. He has a fake rubber hand that can be left protruding from a closed closet door. Coming home from school, I look up at my second-floor bedroom window to see my brother's body hanging there by a rope, but it's his pants and shirt stuffed with laundry.

At night, on the far side of the bed, I see a hand made of flesh. I ease out of the sheets, holding my breath, tiptoe down the stairs to my father's bed. We lie together like spoons. My father jokes about his free arm, that he doesn't know where to put it.

It all changes when I'm seventeen and the Big Goof arrives. He is my first lover. My father pouts and sulks in his big chair. "Tell him you love him," the Big Goof advises. "When you go in tonight, wake him up and tell him you love him." "I love you," I say, crouched on the blanket at the foot of his bed. "What?" my father growls. "I love you." His eyes narrow. "What do you want now?"

The Big Goof, so named by my brother because he is big and his last name is Goff, wears Old Spice and has a fake I.D. He smokes and swears (he says everything but "fuck") and he drinks Scotch. He is a 230-pound All-State tackle. He has friends who wear wide-collared shirts that don't button down and who go out with showgirls. I wear sleek Schiaparelli hose and high heels, and for my eighteenth birthday he gives me a giant stuffed panda and takes me to a motel.

Fifteen years later, when my father hears his name, he grunts. "That son of a bitch!" Fifteen years later, my brother still calls him the Big Goof.

"I promise I won't get into your pants until you're eighteen," he says, but he doesn't make it. It's at a party on Lake Shore Drive, in the bedroom, my black silk Chinese dress with salmon lining pushed up above my waist. The room throbs. I lie on the bed, unsuspecting. The blood. He is pleased at the blood. Where the blood has spread to my dress, the shine has gone out of the silk. He walks to the window; along the torn barbed-wire edge of the screen he rakes his hand until it bleeds. With drama, he reenters the party, blood dripping from his hand, to explain my dress.

Now I am "his" virgin. He buys the most expensive rubbers, the kind that are already wet and have ribs along the sides. We will get married, of course.

Lying on the living room sectional underneath the Big Goof, I hear a noise, a rustle. I follow it around a corner, up the stairs, into the bathroom. My brother is standing, in his size 10 sneakers, fully clothed, behind the shower curtain.

Why doesn't somebody stop it, I don't want to go to college, I have to be under or beside the Big Goof. He wants me to be a Pi Phi. The day I leave him I feel as though my hands have been cut off at the wrists.

On my purple bedspread there is a flesh-colored pool of vomit, its pieces diffuse and undigested. My brother walks silently across the room, his face deadpan; with his thumb and forefinger he picks up the vomit. "Rubber," he says. His lips curl up over his incisors, only the soft corners of his lips participating in the smile.

The Big Goof phones me in the dorm after the switchboard has closed for the night. The housemother, in haircurlers and robe, raps on my door and announces "the emergency." It's Dr. Goff, a routine bed check. Do I belong to him, or am I a whore? For Christmas vacation someone in knee socks and loafers comes home in my place; on St. Patrick's Day we meet secretly and drink champagne for breakfast in the hotel, but I want orange juice. I don't love him, he's not magic. I have to love him. "I'm not a virgin," I'll have to say to someone, sometime, and it will be unacceptable and I don't want to be a nun.

"I don't love you," I say anyway that second summer in his Mercury with no shock absorbers, parked in the Forest Preserves, and he throws himself out of the car, throws himself on the ground, and writhes in the wet leaves, groaning, choking, gasping. "I never told you, a rare disease, the doctor said at any moment I—" His breathing stops, he clutches his throat and his face turns red and swollen, and I stand above him, my arms at my side. I deserve it all, and worse.

And get it. So much later, lying underneath some other lover on the floor, a carpet tack scrapes the skin of my back when he puts his weight on me, pushing me up the rough carpet. Afterwards, there is a round raw spot on the surface of my backbone, bleeding and open, and I have to wrench my body around to admire it in the bathroom mirror. It will heal up, form a scab, and disappear.

In the dark room the yellow light funnels from the television screen. My brother and I are watching Shock Theater. Marvin, the host, is a ghoul dressed in black turtleneck, black pants, and sneakers. Each week he has conversations with Dear, his wife. Week after week, Dear is seated, tied to her chair, her back to the camera, and she is gagged. "Isn't that right, Dear?" Marvin asks, and she mumbles "Help" through her gag, but it comes out like a muffled thud. My brother, his hair cut short in blonde spikes, laughs, throwing his head back, the contours of his face forming upward V's in the dim light.

The first time the Big Goof meets my father, he offers him a light. (He has a gold Dunhill lighter like the one Elizabeth Taylor gives Laurence Harvey in *Butterfield 8.*)

My father rises from his chair and it is settled: the Big Goof must go. So I meet him on corners. My father sets his clock radio every hour on the hour after midnight: Patti Page at two, he checks my bed, Dean Martin at three. At four, he is standing on the porch, fully dressed, smoking Lucky Strikes, his number 5 iron leaning against the screen door. The Big Goof drives over his lawn, leaves tire tracks on his sod.

The Mercury parked in a deserted cul-de-sac, the beam of the policeman's flashlight falls on my chest where the Big Goof's head has been. He flashes his I.D. and says, "This is my fiancee." The wind is cool on our damp skin as we drive naked through the suburban town, the only car on the road.

At the kitchen table, under the bare light, my father offers me $1,000 not to see the Big Goof for one year. My brother hulks, unseen, behind the sliding door.

The Big Goof tells me he will love me no matter what, he will love me if my arms are amputated or my body paralyzed below the waist. He will love me, no matter what—except, maybe, if something happened to my face— (I sit in a gleaming wheelchair, the useless silver armrests kept shining by the Big Goof's muscle, my sleeves empty, my legs hanging from my body like rag dolls, my beautiful face waiting for its own collapse.)

And I will love him because I smell him and breathe him and am surrounded and inundated by him, and I have no choice: if he were a hangnail soaked in Old Spice, if he were a toe—

So what happened? To the beach blankets, their smell of sweat and wool roasting in the sun, turning damp and salty in the evening, so full of us I want to shove them down my throat, and still, and still— The matching yellow monogrammed pajamas we kept hidden in the trunk of his car. The hot leather seat covers steam under my thighs: we are moving. He slams me up against the refrigerator, presses his hands around my neck. I yell "Help" like a muffled thud.

The Night Monster is the worst because he is human, and, better, crippled. His dead legs hidden under a plaid blanket, he rises from his wheelchair into the mist; his legs, stiff as cylinders, move him forward. "Come on, Night, baby!" My brother grins into the TV screen, slices through the center of a kernel of popcorn held tentatively between his front teeth.

I hated seeing him that last time in his Corvette Sting Ray with fuel injection, he is still smelling—reeking—of Old Spice, and I almost reeled, almost. In the motel the

sheets are stretched tight across the bed, cool and crisp
from the air conditioning; we get that far, then I bolt.
Feeling sorry for the money he's spent, sorry he, sorry—
He was big, but his muscles had turned, he was so much
meat.

What am I supposed to do about them? The brother
who loved Frankie, my father with his big bucks and
narrowed eyes, the Big Goof who went soft? The scab,
you can't see a trace of it, but I remember its red amoeba-
like shape, circled in pale yellow, the hint of infection, a
sore, a badge.

Close-Ups

The Number One Idol is dead. His face in the obituary: white hair on white paper. He is smiling, and his eyes veer off the page. I recognize the gaze. I had tried to follow it there, to some sad, precious thing. I try to follow it now, but I stop short, my eyes remaining on the page. I hadn't seen him in twelve years. I hadn't spoken to him. We didn't write. Had he lived twelve years more, I wouldn't have seen him. He never left Ohio, and I wouldn't go back there. So much is made of death; I wonder if it matters. I wonder if it matters whether it is now or was then that he, in his great gray overcoat, walked into the classroom and said, "This is a good day to stay home and eat crackers in bed," and immediately we were all in bed with him, close up to the watercolor-wash blue eyes whose white brows slanted upwards, slightly evil, to those neat ears that lay flat against his head and pointed heavenward, that voice like syrup-over-pebbles in our ears, in our mouths. He died, and I felt like a hatchet had struck my ankles.

My arms wrapped around books, I blow deep into my scarf, wooly breath coming back to warm my face. My legs are bare between knee socks and skirt. The pleats sway, scraping my raw skin. Beside me is my friend Miranda. We walk past the county jail. We walk past the post office and guess which of the old men who laze on its steps have tails hidden in their pants. We walk past the bus station, across Route 23, to the chapel and Haig's eight o'clock. We whisper about our idols. There are semi-idols: a black man with a mustache like sleek cat's tails who wears a starched ROTC uniform; a blonde boy with pale brow and tortured dark eyes whose face we have cut from *Photography Annual*. Haig is the only Full Idol. Number One. Legs crossed in a caduceus, I sit in the middle of the front row, not close enough to his face, to his smile, to his gesturing empty hands. There is a heartbreaking tear in the elbow of his unironed, yellowed shirt. It cries out for us.

After curfew we slip out of the dormitory and sneak to his house, three blocks from where we sleep. We gape at the Victorian monster. In its front window there is a large woman wearing a green bathrobe, ironing. It is her: Clytemnestra. (So he has called her in class.) We giggle, we are so weird, we grab each other's hands, and I feel a chill that cannot be part of our game. I turn from Miranda and run, run three blocks back to the dormitory to the side door we've propped open with a copy of *Clarissa*, and wait, panting, for Miranda.

When it happens, I can't tell Miranda. When it happens, it is no longer a game. When it happens, I don't know the words or the names. His name. I can't call him Dr. Haig. I can't call the Number One Idol just plain Jim. I can't say his name, and if, when we're not alone,

I want to speak to him, I have to tap him on the shoulder or stand right in front of him as if I were addressing a deaf man.

Across the lawn he walks, almost rolls, as though there are ball bearings on the soles of his feet. He is unshaven, a gray-white frost on his cheeks and chin, and he wears a gray overcoat, unbuttoned, that lifts and falls in the wind. His hair is pure white, and very short; it lies close to his head and sticks down in little prongs onto his forehead. He smokes, letting the ash from his cigarette drop onto the front of his coat. "Good morning, Deborah Jane," he says, taking in the campus with a sweep of his hand.

He pulls his Chevy van into the driveway of the wrong house; it is the one next door to where the green woman had been ironing. "What about the neighbors?" I ask. I mean, what about *her*. I mean, promise me I won't be killed.

"The garage is attached to the house," he says. "We'll go straight in from there." On the concrete steps at the door from the garage to the house, he lays his hand on my neck, and, in his face, close up, in the frost on his cheek, in the jowls that have just begun to slacken, I feel his age.

I won't do it in the house. She is all over it. In the books, in the linens, in the worn rugs. She hangs at the hall stairs, as homecoming queen three years before I was born. She has square shoulders and jaunty dark hair. It is twenty-two years later and she has been mad off and on for ten. There are children. The youngest, Nellie, cries from inside her fever, "Stay here and be my mommy." I kiss her at the hairline, run three blocks back to the dormitory where the doors have already locked shut.

The motels are green. Low, flat green shacks on the backroads. The rooms have small square radios with static on every station. We sit crosslegged on the bed, listen to fertilizer commercials, drink Jack Daniels Sour Mash, and play Jotto. The hair on his chest is gray-white; little tufts of white hair spring from his ear lobes. His face is flushed, broken veins in his cheeks like fine pen lines. His dazzling mouth pouts as he sucks on a pencil tip. On the eve of the marriage I make to escape him, he will telephone and breathe one word: "eerie." The perfect Jotto word: three out of five letters are the same.

We hide out in the next county. At a roadhouse, a local is expert at sleight of hand. Haig likes to drink with the broken-down old boys, drinks with the keeper of the county zoo, with the one-eyed postmaster, with this magician whose mean little face has been softened by whiskey. His palm follows the errant fifty-cent piece under the table, behind Haig's shot glass, inside my blouse pocket. Haig buys him a short beer. "And she," he says, nodding toward me, the sliver of his mouth turned up on a grin, "is she your granddaughter?"

"I'm his wife," I say, placing my hand on the table, on the third finger, a dimestore band.

The magician disappears. I talk fast; I can't get to our future too fast: we move to New York City where people are sophisticated, Haig writes a best-selling thriller, we drink and fuck a lot, are rich, happy, and notorious. "No, my love," he says. "Our ending will be like this: I will order you to leave me for your own good, and you'll do it. You'll marry a lawyer" (and the way he says "lawyer" we could lie down in the grass and rest between the syllables) "or, God forbid, a stockbroker, who will support you in the manner to which you were accustomed— before you knew me. You will have two children, each with freckles on his nose like on yours. I only hope you'll remember me with some fondness—"

"No!" I cry. Across the booth, I grab his neck with both hands, press my palms into his skin to firm it.

He writes the first three pages of the thriller.

Someone blabs. Clytemnestra returns from the asylum with names, dates, places. She crashes into the kitchen of the rooms Haig has rented above the campus bookstore. She is large, in a brown coat, and with teeth like pilings of a rotted dock. She stalks the circle of the kitchen table. She walks behind me, puts her hands on the back of my chair, and shoves it, the wooden legs making a shrill scrape on the linoleum. "So this is the one now?" she says. (Will he let her kill me?)

Haig stands with his back to us, at the counter by the sink. We have run out of Jack Daniels and he is pouring cooking sherry into a jelly glass.

She lowers herself into the chair next to me at the table. "You don't think you're the first, do you?"

Haig turns to her, his glorious face awash. He is gray

and tired, and when he speaks there is in his voice too much kindness. "I love her," he says.

Her unkempt face leers close to mine. "What color eyebrow pencil is that you have on, sweetheart?"

"Smoke," I tell her.

I want her to die, I want her to be happy, I want to pack us all off somewhere where it's safe.

"I love you." I run my hand down the jagged scar on his thigh. Bayonet, Italy, World War II. What is a bayonet? I try to remember from the late shows. He rolls down the shot-up Italian hill and is nursed by Italian whores. Anna Magnani. Six months after V-E Day my mother lifts me above the barricades to Eisenhower, who kisses my cheek with his clean, dry lips. We make love eight times. He cooks meatloaf with hunks of potato mixed in, and as I eat he watches me, and smokes and smokes. His emphysema is threatening. Clytemnestra is threatening. The college is threatening. The nuns are threatening to take his small daughters. We sit on borrowed sheets and play Scrabble until it's time to make love again. I win with sure one syllables in play after play while he searches for the single, stunning word.

Clytemnestra takes to passing by campus in the van, trying to run me over. Around every corner I see her, high up at the wheel, a cigarette hanging from the ruins of her teeth. She is driving for blood. She rats on me to my housemother. She rifles the files in the Registrar's Office and grabs my I.Q. She leaks it to him; hers is higher, thus erasing my breasts, their pink nipples, and my smooth thighs. I dream I am onstage at graduation and as the president steps up to hand me my diploma, just as my fingers are about to grasp it, at the edge of the campus lawn she steps down from the van, takes out a rifle, and shoots me through the heart.

The zoo keeper corners me in the bus station. He buys me coffee and says, "You should look up *emphysema* in a medical dictionary in the library. Your man is very sick. He is straining his lungs. He is straining his heart. You stop him drinking! Stop him smoking! Stop him, Deborah Jane, or he'll die." The zoo keeper squats down in the jackal's cage: "Eat roughage for bulk: lettuce, cabbage, a nice cole slaw. All this raw meat's no good for you."

I am backed against the white wall, inches from the door. Haig sits at the kitchen table in the darkening room. The downward lines in his face turn black as the face lights up in the flame of the kitchen matches he strikes, one by one, and flicks at me. His chest heaves. His shirt is unironed, is ill-buttoned, one tail hanging inches below the other. His face is florid, his cheeks heavy, his blue eyes, slits. We glare at each other. Neither of us can move.

The cross-examination:
Q. Do you love him?
A. Yes.
Q. Will you stay with him?
A. Yes. No.
Q. Well?
A. Yes I've poured myself into him and left nothing over. No he's skipping to the grave and pulling me alongside—

Q. Yes or no?
A. I have one foot on either side of a gaping split in the quake-reft ground, my legs are spreading wider and wider—
Q. Yes or no? Yes or no? Yes or no?

Haig and I sit in a rowboat in the middle of a green lake. He has let the oars lie slack in their sockets. I am wearing a smock with tiny pink flowers on ivory, two pigtails and bare feet. Haig's gray cuffs slosh in the water in the hull of the boat. He has worn the same shirt for three days: yellowed white. His face is yellow-white, set on his shoulders like a bloated moon. He coughs, takes a swig of Big Cat, coughs again. Underneath me, the hard seat seesaws with the undulations of the water. I dive into the thick green lake, swim in quick, clean strokes, and surface where the boat is a yellow speck between water and sky.

After Haig's death, I dream a portfolio of his papers has been forwarded to me in the mail. It includes a book he has written: I can't see the title, but the dustjacket is shiny and smooth and green, and on the back cover, in a black and white photograph, is Haig, in his gray over-coat, walking, springing, on his ball-bearing feet; as he goes forward off the page, his face, glorious again, is three-quarters turned back, smiling at me.

Notes

Sally looks up at Barry. He's wearing a pair of white ducks that are ripped all the way up the crotch. He likes loose clothes, clothes several sizes too big for him. He doesn't like to button or zip; things are more comfortable that way. He opens his mouth big and wide, leans over Sally wide-eyed and expectant, waggles his tongue at her, and hums: "Ahhhhhhhhh."

Sally stands before him, pleading. She feels her jeans have grown too tight. Her streaked hair looked brassy this morning. Barry said it did. At least he agreed with her. Now he is looking right at her, waiting. He is a musician, and he wants to test her ear. He wants Sally to copy the note he's humming. She's afraid she won't get it right, and then Barry will come to her laughing and kiss her all over her face and say, "That's pathetic, baby."

"Ahhhhhhhh." Barry puts his hands on his hips, smiles broadly, takes a deep breath. "Ahhhhhhh. Ahhhhhhhhhhhh. Come on, baby. It's only middle C."

Sally wriggles. "I can't." She's thinking about something he did to her when they were married. He had leaned over her in bed, taken her hands into his, and made her hit her own face with her hands. His mouth was open, his upper lip drawn back so she could see his gums. She lay back and felt her own hands slap her face.

Now she turns her back to Barry. He comes up behind

her, puts his arms around her, and shakes her. "Baby, baby, why can't you do it? I'm the only one here."

They're not sure how it happened this way, but Barry lives in Boston and Sally lives in New York. Sally is going to take the five o'clock shuttle back to New York to meet Gerald, and Janice expects Barry home for dinner in Brookline at six. Barry and Sally both hate motels, but they have just made love in one. Barry is sitting on the edge of the bed with his jacket open, waiting. He looks up at Sally. He watches her closely. She picks up packs of motel matches, first from the night table between the two beds, then from the desk, then from the ashtray in the bathroom. She puts the matches in her purse. "Baby!" Barry cries. "How can you think of matches at a time like this?"

"I need matches," Sally says. Barry's eyes are glazed and his lower lip is slack. She sees he is accusing her. She opens one of the matchboxes to show him. "They're especially good matches. Wooden."

"But, baby. How can you even *notice* matches?"

The bed is below two windows. The morning sun pushes through the shades onto Barry and Sally sleeping. Sally groans, turns her body towards Barry, and thrashes her legs against the sheets. She turns her head from side to side, eyes closed, face to the sun. Barry reaches to her and puts his hand over her eyes to shade them from the sun. His hand is cool.

Barry has hypoglycemia. He isn't supposed to drink. He is supposed to eat protein every three hours. Sally has promised she will cure him with high protein milkshakes, soybean powder, dessicated liver tablets, but she hasn't gotten to the health food store yet. At the liquor store she bought two bottles of wine, and she and Barry are in her apartment drinking it.

Sally is saying: "You know, that couple? He was a sportswriter, and I told her she looked like Barbra Streisand, and she said, 'Barbra Streisand is a great talent, but I happen to think she's one of the ugliest women alive.'"

"I don't remember, baby," Barry says.

"Come on, Barry, they lived in Pompano Beach—"

"Oh, yeah. Steven."

"Do you still see him?"

"Uh, last spring we—" Barry stops. He can't say *we*. Not to her. Because *we* is Barry and the woman he lived with for the seven years he and Sally have been divorced. He starts the sentence again. "I drove down to see them, and they didn't even offer me a sandwich. I wanted to spend the night, but Steven said his wife got nervous with someone else in the house, using the same bathroom." Barry looks at Sally as if to say, "Can you imagine such a thing?"

"I can't imagine such a thing," Sally says.

"We were, like, friends for life, and then I can't even piss in his bathroom."

Sally and Barry look across the table into each other's eyes. "*We're* not like that," they don't have to say.

Sally takes a swallow of wine. She doesn't blame Steven's wife for not wanting Janice's kid around, messing up her house.

Barry and Sally are walking to Barry's Volkswagen. Sally isn't wearing gloves. She walks huddled into her coat with her hands thrust down into the pockets. Her teeth are chattering, and she is letting out a low moan.

Lying on the front seat of Barry's car is a pair of wool mittens. Sally reaches for them.

Barry looks down at his lap. He takes a deep breath. His voice is solemn. "I don't know if I can let you wear those."

Sally drops the mittens. She looks at Barry.

"Janice gave them to me."

Sally sees the struggle on Barry's face. He wants to do the right thing. The right thing by Sally and the right thing by Janice.

He looks at Sally. His eyes are wet. "Oh, baby, go ahead. Wear them. Your hands are cold. Of course you should wear them." He takes her hands in his. His hands are warm.

"I can't baby. I can't find a place to live. I'm sleeping at Raphael's, the bassist's place. Baby, he has bags of garbage all over. The roaches travel from bag to bag. You know how I feel about showers. I can't live without a good shower, and the water comes out brown. The radiator is broken. I'm freezing my ass off. Of course there's no piano."

"So get your own place and move your piano into it," Sally says. She scratches at her arms. They have broken out in hives during the telephone conversation. There is a big red splotch below her collarbones, rising up her neck. She's watching the clock on top of the refrigerator. It's a long-distance call, and Barry reversed the charges.

"I can't."

"Why not?"

"It's not my piano. It's rented. Janice rents it for me."

"Rents? Rents? Do you mean she still has it?" Sally wants to be sexy and oblivious, but when she talks to Barry she sounds like a lawyer.

"Yeah."

"Why?"

"I don't know, baby, what difference does it make?"

"Does *she* play the piano?"

"No."

"Barry. If Janice doesn't play the piano and she still has the piano it means she expects you back—"

"Baby! You sound like a lawyer."

"—and, oh shit, Barry, if she expects you back it's because you haven't made it clear you're not coming back. Goddamn it, Barry, we're going to blow it. We're going to blow it *again*."

"Baby, how can you say that? Don't say that. Did you hear what you said? I couldn't bear that, baby. It would kill me. This is our last chance. I'm thirty, this is the Big Time, baby, you and I know that. You're everything. We're everything."

"So get an apartment."

"It's not that easy."

Sally wants the chaise that's facing the sun. She picks up a pair of sunglasses from it and puts them on an empty chair and lies down. She is sunburned all over except where her straps were. It's her last day in Florida so she wants her strapmarks tanned. She wraps herself in beach towels from her feet to her shoulders. Only the tops of her shoulders show. She is wearing sunglasses, Noxzema on her nose, and a scarf over her hair. She watches a young man climb out of the pool and walk

towards her chaise. She thinks he's about her age, twenty-
two, but maybe he's older because he's so hairy, and maybe
he's younger because he's so slight. She thinks he's older
because there's something kind of slick about him. He
looks like no one she's ever seen except maybe certain
stand-up comics. "I moved your glasses," she says.

Barry picks up his glasses. He sits down and throws
his head back, his wet face to the sun.

"I took your chair," Sally says.

She is smiling. Barry can't see much of her. She is
covered with towels. She is smiling. Her teeth are good.

That night they sit in Barry's car outside a motel. "I
want to spend the night with you," he says. "But I don't
have enough cash. Want to pay half of the motel bill?"

"Are you kidding?"

"No. Why should I be?"

Sally is silent.

"Twenty bucks is a lot of bread."

Sally is silent.

"I'm only a student, babe."

Barry slumps against the front door on the driver's
side, taps his long fingers on his knee, scats to the tune
of "Satin Doll." Sally slumps over herself, feet up on the
dashboard, head on arms on knees. She yawns.

"Whew." Barry blows out a long breath like a whistle.
"Okay, baby. I'll pay. Just loan me ten until tomorrow."

Sally turns to him, smiles. "How do I know you'll pay
me back?"

He tosses his watch into Sally's lap. "Solid gold," he
says.

Eight years later Barry and Sally are in bed. Barry has
drunk too much wine for his hypoglycemia and Sally

has drunk more. She's lying on her back, and Barry is curled up next to her, whispering in her ear. "Are you sure you're awake?"

Sally rolls her head to one side. Her eyelids flutter. "Uh huh."

"O kaaaaay. So listen, baby. Are you listening? Tell me if you're not. Hmnnnnn. I guess if you're not listening you can't tell me. I don't want to get into a whole rap with you if you're asleep. Are you listening?"

"Ummnnn."

"You better be, baby. I'm going to give you a quiz tomorrow morning. I'm thinking about our life, baby. I see it this way: music and fucking. I roll out of bed at four in the morning, compose a tune on the piano—when we have a piano, that is—a tune that's been running through my head all night while I'm asleep, and you wake up when you hear me playing. You raise yourself up on one elbow, and you are really beautiful, sleepy, like now, only your eyes are open, and the tune stones you out, of course. OF COURSE. Then we make love. Just because it's night we don't have to sleep, see? It's out of time, baby. It's like jazz. It's like—. Baby. Are you sure you're awake?"

"How are we going to live?"

"Huh?"

Sally takes a deep breath. "Money."

Barry rolls over onto his elbow and looks up at Sally. Chick Corea is doing a riff on RVR, and Barry lets out a low whistle. "Can he play. *Wails.*" Another low whistle. He takes a strand of Sally's hair and rubs it between his thumb and forefinger, looks up at her and smiles. "Sorry, baby. What did you ask me about?"

"Money."

Barry drops his hand from Sally's hair. "What about money, baby, besides I don't have any and never will?"

"How are we going to live?"

"Oh, baby, are you still so materialistic? If you just, like, follow your instincts, when you need money it'll turn up."

Sally is not used to the gas stove that has to be lighted each time by putting a match down into a hole at the bottom of the oven. She turns on the gas without lighting the pilot light. Barry smells the gas.

"Oh shit," Sally says. "I forgot to light the oven again."

Barry looks at her. His face is stern. His voice is soft. "You could kill yourself, baby, when I'm not here."

Sally shrugs.

Barry goes into the kitchen. He takes a pack of matches and a roll of scotch tape. He tapes the pack of matches to the dial that turns on the gas.

Sally dreams she is sitting at the edge of a clear pool with Barry. His body, hips to feet, is covered with scales that shine through the water. His back is smooth and soft like a young boy's. She strokes the smooth soft skin on his back. He feels young. He is maybe ten, and she is a woman; she expects things.

Barry tells Sally his dream: he dreams someone is knocking at his door. Janice's son is with him. Barry opens the door and is knocked down. A gun is thrust into his back. He feels his wallet being slipped out of his pants. The mugger takes the hand of Janice's little boy and leads him through the doorway. Barry looks up from the floor to see the face of the mugger: it's Sally. In his sleep, Barry screams into his pillow. Sally reaches over to stroke his smooth, soft back.

Sally is falling asleep. Barry caresses her neck. Her breath catches. Barry leaves his hand on her neck, turns to the wall at the side of the bed. "For seven years I woke up at night without you, and I longed for you. Now you're here, and I still long for you." His hand slips off her neck.

Sally sees Barry's white body coming toward her, raised above her on the mattress, lowering itself towards her. It looks like a headlight in a dark night, like a gull's wing, not like flesh, and she lashes out at him, screams no-nononono. He collapses back, hugs his arms around his chest, and stares at her: her wild eyes, her face flushed in the candlelight, the blue sheet clutched between her breasts. The white candle is slight, gives a wavering light to the whole dark room. He watches it burn down, feels the warm wax run over his fingertips, then rubs it between his thumb and forefinger.

Barry sits on the toilet, elbows on knees, staring into the hall. Sally stands over him, combing her hair in the medicine chest mirror. She hears the stream of urine. She remembers how when they were married he would stand at the sink, shaving, his limp penis resting on the edge.

"Why don't you piss standing up?"

Barry looks at her sideways and sighs. "It's less strenuous sitting down. Do you think I'm any less a man because I piss sitting down?"

"No," she lies.

I would give anything I own
Give up my life, my heart, my home
I would give everything I own
Just to have you back again
Just to touch you once again

It's raining and the static has blocked out the jazz station. "Bread" is playing on the car radio. Sally sings along with the words. The words are dumb. They make her nauseous, but she sings along anyway. When the song is over, she keeps hearing the words just the same. She is aware of herself and Barry as if they were in a movie: she and Barry in his Volkswagen on the slick highway in the rain in the dark. Cut to flashback: she and Barry in his Chevy Supersport, empty highway, gray morning. They are driving away from the motel eight years ago. Barry says, mock-serious, "This is a portentous day." Pan to gray empty sky.

Barry and Sally are sitting, their backs to the wall, on the floor in the apartment he has sublet. Barry puts his head on his knees and blacks out for a few seconds. When he comes to, he goes to the refrigerator and takes out a piece of bread and spreads cottage cheese on it for protein. The cottage cheese smells a little sour. He stares at Sally, takes a big bite out of the bread, and swallows it without chewing. "You—" Barry starts.

Sally is filing her nails. "What?"

Barry puts the bread on the floor. "I can't say it. It's too horrible."

Sally pushes up her sweater sleeve and scratches her arm where it's starting to itch again. "What?"

"You don't make a home for me."

"Neither do you."

Barry tells Sally he brings candy bars over to Janice's son, and Janice lets Barry play the baby grand.

Sally tells Barry she lets Gerald take her out to dinner, but she doesn't let him touch her except when she can't help it.

"Gerald said he'd take me to Marrakesh," Sally says.

"Janice said she'd take me to L.A. for primal therapy. The full course."

It is Barry and Sally's wedding day. Barry's suit is too big. He hasn't worn it since his grandfather's funeral. He hasn't thought to send it to the cleaner's, and it's wrinkled. Sally hasn't thought to buy a dress for her wedding, so she's wearing her mother's blue suit which is three sizes too big. She's rolled the skirt up at the waist. Her shoes are too tight. They pinch. She has piled her hair on top of her head, but it has come out from the bobbie pins and fallen down her back. There's a football in the back seat of the car, and Barry and his brother run for passes in the parking lot until it's time for Barry and Sally to go inside and get married.

"I couldn't bear it, never to feel your skin again, never to smell you, the smell of your breath, your skin, your urine." Barry moans, his mouth on Sally's ear, his breath on her cheeks; her hair streams onto his eyes, her tears wet the hollows in his face. They are sitting on a bench, waiting for the shuttle.

"It isn't working," Sally whispers.

"It has to. You're always leaving me, baby. I feel like you've been leaving me all my life."

Sally rubs her eyes with the back of her hand and wipes her hand on her hair. Barry takes her wet hair and brushes it across his face. Sally smiles. She puts her finger on his Adam's apple, feels it hard, pulsating underneath her fingertip. Barry smiles. Sally's face is red and wet and throbbing.

"We'll do something, baby," Barry says.

Sally kisses the spot where his two front teeth overlap. "Like what?"

They have been married for five months. In two more, they will be divorced. Sally is lying beside the pool in the apartment building parking lot exchanging Polack jokes with some man. Barry is upstairs in the apartment, trying to compose. He can see Sally down by the pool, laughing. She can see Barry come downstairs, get into the Supersport, and drive away. She sees him come back and go upstairs with a grocery bag in his arms. When she goes up to the apartment, he is sitting at the table eating a TV dinner.

"Where's mine?" Sally asks.

Barry doesn't look up. "I only bought one."

Sally says she's going to the K-Mart, but she spends the night getting drunk and going to bed with the man from the pool. She doesn't want Barry to worry, so she calls him to tell him she's all right. Barry turns over all the furniture in the apartment and flushes her birth control pills down the toilet.

". . . man and wife."

Barry and Sally kiss. Arms around each other in their too-big clothes they kiss until the judge pulls them apart.

"Oh, Barry, please forgive me. Forgive me. I love you. I didn't mean to hurt you—"

Sally is on her knees at the side of the bed. Barry is sitting above her on the bed. He watches her. His eyes are wide and glassy. "I don't believe you."

"Barry!"

"You're an actress. You're acting a part. But I don't believe it."

Sally feels foolish on her knees.

Will you be the one to give birth to me?
If not, oh, well, we'll see

are the last words of the last song Barry writes for Sally. He tapes it so he can mail it to her, but he leaves it in his desk for a long time. He's afraid she'll laugh, he tells her. He mails it, but when Sally receives it, it takes her a long time to find a machine to play it on because everyone has cassettes by now. The song isn't what she expected; it's not what she expected at all. At the end, Barry's voice is tentative, reaching, the last note dissonant and stretched out.

L.A.

I know it's a mistake when I get off the plane in L.A. The plane isn't late, and it isn't early, so there's no reason for Ben not to be here. He isn't here. I get on a moving sidewalk that takes me to the baggage claim. I see Ben, but he doesn't see me. "Ben!" I call out.

At least, I think it's Ben. When we were in New York together he didn't have his black hair rolling down past his shoulders, and he wasn't wearing a Stetson.

The moving sidewalk drops me at his feet. "Ben!" I cry. I jump up to kiss him. He is very tall and doesn't look down. He doesn't pick up my suitcase. We haven't seen each other for six months. We haven't lived together for more than that, and when we did it was awful. But things got even worse. So I called Ben long distance and invited myself to L.A. I figured we were about the best either of us was going to end up with.

Ben looks over my head around the airport as if he's expecting to meet someone. Then he looks down at me.

"Did you come straight from work?" he asks.

He is looking at my Paraphernalia shirtdress and Italian patent leather high-heeled sandals. He hopes it's a compulsory nine-to-five costume. "Yes," I lie. I didn't know everyone on the Coast was dressing like cowboys and Indians.

"No one wears bras out here," Ben tells me.

"Take me with you!" I had cried the night before Ben left for L.A. We were sitting at a table in the Dug-Out on Bleecker Street. Two years ago, in '67, the Dug-Out was SRO with all of us sitting around watching the door for Dylan to come in. He never did. Now the place was empty.

Ben smiled a sweet smile. "I can't," he said. "There's no room in my car."

I was living with someone else anyway. So Ben's suit-case instead of me rode in the front seat of the Lotus up the West Side Highway, across the George Washington Bridge to L.A. I stayed in the Village and wondered where everyone had gone. I had made a big mistake not holding on to Ben. I couldn't find another man who didn't make me feel guilty.

"I'm known for my car," Ben says as he steps over the side into the driver's seat. His Lotus is a low black roach of a car that rides six inches off the ground. I can hear the tires whine on the freeway and feel the loose stones strike the metal underbelly. I need to be alone with Ben. Then everything will be all right.

A few miles up the Canyon he pulls into a parking lot. A sign says THE CORRAL.

"Everybody goes here," Ben says.

I follow him into the club. The car has no trunk or top, so I carry my suitcase inside. There are clusters of girls sitting on the steps. Blonde, tan, and braless, they look like California fruit. In California you can get ripe fruit anywhere, year-round. There's a big turnover, so it never goes rotten. I feel like a winter tomato left over on the produce shelf in a New York A&P.

Ben looks over the place like John Wayne looking over the Northwest Territory. I stand behind him, acutely aware of my good posture. "Hey!" he yells. He goes up to a table and pulls up a chair. I pull up a chair, too. No one makes room for us, so I hold my beer on my lap. Ben's friends at the table are wearing torn jeans, old shirts, and sandals. They all look sleepy. Ben leans forward towards them. "Joanie just flew in from New York," he says. He says it loud and clear so no one can miss it. His voice saying my name jolts me.

"Far out," one of the guys says. He blows smoke from his cigarette which he holds between his thumb and forefinger like a joint.

Ben drums his fingers on the table. "When's the next set? The whole group here? I heard the bass player got busted in the Valley last night."

The guy who said "far out" shrugs.

Ben takes a long pull on his beer and tips his chair back. "Great place, isn't it?"

The lead singer gets up from a table and mounts the stage. It's a girl. She has waist-length blonde hair that frizzes into the spotlight. She is wearing tight Western pants, cowboy boots, and an Indian belt with turquoises the size of eggs.

Ben leans close to me. "See her? I wanted to manage her, but she's flipped out. Didn't show up for the recording session to make a demo. She'll never make it."

The group starts up. I stare at Ben's face and at the faces around the table. I feel like I'm in a movie set of a Western town. It looks like a Western town, but when you walk up to one of the houses, the door doesn't open, and you can't see anything through the windows. I try to remember what I'm doing in L.A.

I'm still trying to remember when the lead singer thrusts the mike out between her thighs, yanks it back as if she were pulling in the reins of a horse. She tosses her hair forward over her head, slashes her arm down from above her head to her feet, throws her electric yellow frizzed hair to her knees, gives one stomp with her boot heel, and the set is over.

It was the last set.

Ben looks depressed.

His house is farther up the Canyon. His brass bed, his gargoyles, his chair with the lion's face carved in the wood are there. Moved from the Village to Soho to L.A. They look strange here, civilized, in the wilderness, in his one-room house set into the side of a hill. His thin Persian rugs lie on a dirt floor. I drop my clothes and get into bed. I want to sleep. Ben and I haven't spoken on the ride up the Canyon. Maybe tomorrow we'll wake up and something will happen between us.

Ben gets out of his clothes and climbs on top of me.

"I have to get up," I say.

"Huh?"

"To get my diaphragm."

"Forget it." Ben rolls off me. "All the chicks out here take the pill."

"I gave it up with the cancer scare," I say.

He yawns.

It's six in the morning in New York. I hear the airplane

engines, the electric guitars, the engine of the Lotus. I smell the grass and the Marlboros and the warm beer. I see the lead singer's yellow frizzed hair, hear Ben's voice: "Did you come straight from work?"

I want to sleep, but I see flashes of Ben and me in New York: Ben brings home a cake that says HAPPY AN-NIVERSARY; it was on sale at the bakery; someone forgot to pick it up. We get stoned and eat the whole cake, celebrating someone else's anniversary. Ben rubs his cheek on my shoulder and makes little whining sounds like a dog, his eyes closed, his lips smiling. It is my birthday and he comes out of the bathroom with a pink ribbon tied around his erect penis. We lie in bed. It is raining, and the wet leaves from the tree in the courtyard push through the window onto our pillow. They smell damp and fresh. Ben's chest is damp, and my head lies on it. I feel his chest rise and fall. The damp hairs on his chest tickle my cheek.

These scenes punctuated by Ben's snores from the other side of the bed.

In the morning Jake walks in through the sliding glass doors and stands at the side of the bed. I knew Jake in New York. He and his wife were a folk-singing duo before they came to L.A. Then they split up. Ben and I and Jake and his wife hung out together even though his wife didn't like me. I looked too much like Sylvia Tyson, she said. She and Jake had a great apartment on Bleecker Street for $76 a month. Now Jake lives in his VW bus in Ben's driveway.

Jake rubs his eyes and blinks. "She's gone," he says.

Ben groans. "Who?"

"My chick. She split—"

"Later," Ben says.

Ben is working in Hollywood producing somebody's Greatest Hits. "If you want to go anywhere you can hitch," he tells me when he leaves. "All the chicks hitch around here."

"Not me. Manson was caught only last week. He might have friends."

Ben frowns, then smiles. "Hey! Charlie and the family used to live here. In this house. My house. A couple of years ago!"

I open my suitcase. My diaphragm is packed on top. I take out my bikini. I am New York pale. I take my paperback and go to lie in the sun. I need to look more like something the Beach Boys sing about and less like something Antonioni puts in empty rooms with white walls. That was okay in New York, even good, but in L.A. it's nonnegotiable.

Jake pulls into the driveway in his bus. He has picked up someone named Miller and his old lady, Moon. They all sit down next to me, and Miller starts talking.

"I'm into interrelationships, like the sun and the moon—"

Jake stares at the grass. "She split, man. To Malibu. With a surfer."

"—the Cosmos. I got my Ph.D. back East. In philosophy. Hah! A couple thousand micrograms of acid was my education." Miller keeps talking. I sneak glances at the book on my lap. He doesn't seem to notice.

After a while, Moon goes into the house. I realize she hasn't said anything.

"Is she all right?" I ask Miller.

"What do you mean?"

"She doesn't talk."

Miller smiles. "Oh, yeah. I get you. She's spacey. That's why we call her Moon." Miller leans closer to me. "Tell you what happened. Her father had a thing for her. Wanted to, you know, sleep with her. She came to me for advice. Lots of chicks do. I'm a kind of guru to a lot of chicks. I'm very heavily into the whole Eastern scene, meditation—"

"So what about Moon?"

"Yeah. I told her to sleep with him. It's 1969. We can do anything."

Jake passes Miller a joint. He takes a toke and passes it to me. I take a toke to be polite.

"Columbia?" Miller asks Jake. Jake nods.

"So did she?" I ask Miller.

"Sure. She slept with him. He's a good-looking dude. Old, though." Miller blows out a long stream of smoke. "That's good stuff you got me smoking, Jake."

"And then what?"

"And then nothing. She doesn't talk. That's all."

"Jesus—"

"Ummn. He makes it. Was into the right things—"

"My chick split," Jake says. "She took my guitar."

"Aren't you worried about Moon?" I ask Miller.

"Nah. She's cool. You from New York where everybody's still caught up in logic and rhetoric, you've got to learn to give in. Give it all up. Moon's at peace."

"How do you know?"

Miller runs his thumb through the pages of my paper-back. "Whew. See what I mean? You are still reading books. It's hopeless, even talking to anyone who reads books. Right, Jake?"

Jake looks up from the ground. "I had that guitar since my first gig at the Gaslight in '63."

Ben's Lotus pulls into the driveway. "Blind Faith," he shouts from the car. "They're breaking up. The groups are dead. We're going back to the fifties. Carl Perkins. Buddy Holly. Presley. That's where it's at."

"Buddy Holly's dead," I say.

"So what? He can be re-released."

Ben puts Johnny Cash and Dylan's "Nashville Skyline" on the stereo. "Listen to this intro," he says. "Put on the headphones." He takes the record off and puts on Jimi Hendrix. "Listen to the bridge." He takes it off and puts on Neil Diamond. "Just the note after the drums." He yells over the music. He has speakers the size of the ones in Philharmonic Hall.

I can't think of anything to say. Ben turns off the set and walks out onto the porch. He stares down into the Canyon. "Gotta go," he says. "Have to meet someone in the Valley."

Ben and I go to dinner at Jack and Michelle's in Holly-wood Hills. Jack is Ben's older brother. He is a protest singer-songwriter who made it on the War. Michelle is my roommate from college in Ohio. They live together.

"Am I glad you're here," Michelle says. She takes me into the kitchen where she is chopping garlic for the spareribs. "The last chick Ben brought here was an eighteen-year-old starlet who rides topless in a grade-B motorcycle flick. I have no one to talk to out here. I got an orgone box, so I talk to it every morning. It helps." There is a gold-edged tray table on one of the kitchen counters. "What is that?" I ask Michelle. "Oh. Jack likes to have his breakfast served to him in bed every morning. I eat alone in here."

Jack comes into the kitchen. "The war is a bore," he says. He takes a bottle of Mexican beer from the refrigerator.

"Aren't you going to say hello to Joanie?" Michelle asks.

Jack doesn't look at me or Michelle. He throws his head back. "Where's Ben?" he yells.

Ben comes into the kitchen. "Got any grass, Jack?"

"The revolution got lost, Benjamin," Jack says. "*I am the only one left.*"

"You are a has-been, Jack," Ben says.

"Ah hah, Benjamin. But *you* are a nobody. *I* was a star, Benjamin. *You* were *my* brother. That's all."

Jack and Ben go into the living room to watch the news.

Ronald Reagan's face is greenish-yellow on the color TV. He is having a picnic with some farm workers. "Faggot movie star," Jack says to the screen. Jack is drinking from a bottle of tequila.

"Pass me the bottle, Jack," Ben says.

"No. It's mine." Across the living room there is a pet monkey in a cage. Jack takes the bottle over to him. "Want a drink, Ché?" he says to the monkey. "Come on. You and I are the only ones left." He opens the door to the cage. The monkey swings out and tears up the drapes. It sits on the curtain rod, screeching.

"Christ," Michelle says. "That damn monkey shits all over the place." She opens another bottle of California rosé. "It's cheap out here," she says. "And you can even buy it in the supermarket."

Ben is taking me to an important party in the Valley. It is being given by a folksinger he knew in the Village and her husband who is the road manager for an MOR rock group. The folksinger calls at the last minute and asks Ben if he can pick up a famous rock singer on his way down the Canyon because the rock singer's car doesn't start and his cycle is in the shop. "What a break," Ben says to me. "I want you to wear jeans." I put on jeans and a T-shirt. "Are those real jeans?" he asks. I look down at my legs. "Are they Levis or Lee Riders?"

"They're jeans. They're denim—"

Ben looks away from me. He looks hurt. I look down at my jeans. The denim doesn't seem to lay right on my thighs. It hasn't bleached enough. Ben buys his jeans six months ahead of time and has a friend wear them for him before he'll put them on.

Ben looks in the mirror and adjusts the angle of his Stetson. "Do you like this shirt?" he asks without looking at me. He is wearing a rose-colored Western shirt. "It matches the lenses in my glasses, see?"

"And the color of your lips."

"What?"

"It matches the color of your lips."

"Hey," he says. He pouts into the mirror. "Right." He puts on his beloved leather Wyatt Earp coat that he found in an antique store on the lower East Side. He shifts his torso around in the jacket, claps the pockets. His hands make a resonant sound against the leather.

A mile down the Canyon, Ben pulls into a parking lot. There are a couple of stores and a health food restaurant. He lights a cigarette and turns up the radio. "We're early," he says. "We don't want to be early. It wouldn't look good." He smokes fast and raps his fist on the steering wheel. "Russ Tamblyn hangs out here." He points to the health food restaurant.

"Russ Tamblyn? I remember him from *Hit the Deck*. I had a crush on him. I sent away for his picture. But I was just a kid. He must be old now."

"He's not old."

"He has to be. I was in sixth grade."

"Well, he's not old."

We pull up in front of the rock singer's house. Ben looks into the rear-view mirror and slicks his hair back behind his ears. He steps over the side of the car, pulls up on his Western belt, and rocks back on his bootheels. Then he turns and walks toward the house.

"Ben!" I call.

His head jerks around. "Huh?"

"Nothing."

Ben comes walking down the drive with the rock singer. The rock singer has one arm around Ben's shoulder, but Ben isn't smiling. The rock singer is talking fast and waving his hands.

"Come on, Ben," he's saying when they get to the car. "I'm a star. I need a coat like that. Let me try it on, man."

"Sure thing," Ben says. He shrugs out of his coat. The

singer puts it on. He strides up and down in front of the car. He is too thin. Maybe he is on speed. Ben's coat is too big across the shoulders and chest. He shoves his fists down into the pockets. "Fits great," he says. "Was meant for me. What do you say, man? Your coat plays the Santa Monica Civic Center. How about it?"

Ben is looking at the ground.

"Ben. I'll give you a thousand. You fly to New York, pick up another coat, fly back the same day."

"It's an antique," I say. "He can't get another one. Anywhere."

Ben glares at me.

"What'd the chick say?" the singer asks Ben. "So is it a deal?"

"Sure thing," Ben says.

The singer reaches into his jeans pocket. "You take American Express? Nah, I'll give you a check. My credit's good, man."

"Forget it," Ben says. "It's yours." He laughs, but the laugh doesn't make it to the corners of his mouth.

All the way to the Valley, Ben and the rock singer are laughing and clapping each other on the back, passing a joint back and forth. We pull into the drive at the party and the rock singer goes quiet. Before Ben can get his key out of the ignition, the rock singer is out of the car and headed up the lawn. "Hey, do you need a ride back?" Ben calls out after him. But the rock singer doesn't turn around.

At the party the men are sitting on the patio drinking screwdrivers. The women are sitting in the kitchen. Through the sliding glass doors they can watch the men sitting on the patio. When we walk in, no one says hello.

Ben starts to sweat. He points toward one of the men. His mouth is right at my ear. "See that guy? He writes songs for Pat Boone. He's making it—"

"Pat Boone is an asshole," I say.

"—That guy over there sings in The Corporation. He's made it. That guy he's talking to has a single on the charts this week. 38 with a bullet in Cashbox. 40 in Billboard. That chick? She used to sing at peace rallies. She's a has-been." Ben's face looks pale yellow. He sits down on the edge of a chaise. "Go talk to the chicks," he says.

I go into the kitchen. They are talking about the Hollywood Health Club. "Peggy Lipton goes there," someone says.

I pretend I came in to borrow a cigarette. I go back to Ben. He looks lonely. "Talk to the chicks," he says under his breath. "Be friendly for once."

I go back into the kitchen. I am prepared to say that Pearl Bailey goes to the Hudson Health Club in New York, and we sit in the same sauna. But now they're talking about some macrobiotic restaurant in the Valley that Warren Beatty goes to.

The guy who sings in The Corporation organizes a volleyball game. Ben is the first one on the lawn. I'm sitting on the patio, pretending to read a copy of *Rolling Stone*. Ben comes over. "What's wrong with you?" he whispers. "Get up. We're all playing volleyball."

"I hate volleyball," I say.

"Come on. Play." He says it through his teeth.

I follow Ben to the lawn. We pass the rock singer, who is lying on a chaise looking at the sky. "Volleyball sucks," he says to no one.

"Right," Ben says, turning to him. "But what can I do? Got to be polite."

I play across the net from Ben next to the singer from The Corporation. Ben is watching me. I try to stay away from the ball. I miss my first serve. I miss my second serve. My fist doesn't even touch the ball. Quickly and I hope with a look of purpose I move around in my position, trying to make it look as though it's impossible for me to return the ball. From the other side of the net, Ben is watching me. The singer from The Corporation yells, "I can't play two positions!"

Ben's face is black. I know I'm going to get it.

Jake drives me down to Venice to see an old friend of mine and Michelle's. Bunny left her husband and son in the Village and came to the Coast with her old man. Her old man is nineteen. At our college in Ohio, Bunny had the highest score ever on the English GRE's.

She is tan, and her hair is bleached white. She is wearing a dress she has made out of an Indian print bedspread. Other Indian print bedspreads cover beds and hang on walls. The first thing she says when she sees me is, "What time were you born?"

She sits down and consults some thick books with charts and columns of numbers. "How's Ben?" she asks.

"Okay," I lie. "For Ben."

"What's his sign?"

I wish she wouldn't ask me questions about Ben. "Pisces," I say.

"Pisces with Virgo?" she says. "Well, opposites attract. At first, anyway."

With colored pens she draws little figures on a circle.

"See?" she says. "These are your planets. Look how they're all bunched up in the upper left-hand corner of the chart. It's very unusual. Are you sure you have your time right? Because all these planets are in mental signs. You must think all the time. You might think so much that you never act."

Bunny's old man comes in from the beach. He is wearing a short Indian print cloth wrapped around his hips. His hair is tied back in a ponytail. He is playing a recorder. He doesn't stop to say anything.

Bunny stirs some grass into the vegetable stew. "He makes recorders," she says. "And sells them on the beach."

"Do you sell a lot of them?" I ask.

"Two," he says. "So far."

Ben and I are not making it. I hope he doesn't notice.

There are two pink tablets in Ben's open hand. "Mescaline," he says. "Pure organic California mesc." He swallows one tab with his coffee and hands me the other. "Take it. We'll go down to Malibu."

I haven't taken drugs since the chromosome scare. I want to have a baby, and I don't want my kid's chromosomes to get messed up just so I can see trees change color and tables dance. On the other hand, Ben hasn't screwed me since I got to L.A., so I might never have a baby anyway. (I'm always thinking.)

We fly down the Canyon in the Lotus. "The trees and rocks and flowers look like liquid velvet," I say.

"Hey. That'd be a good name for a group."

I'm pretty sure everything's going to be okay.

The sand undulates to the water's edge. The blue waves fold on top of each other onto the sand. The sand and sky pulsate with life. I am incredibly high. Ben and I are going to make it after all.

"What a rip-off." Ben pounds his fist on the sand. "I can't feel anything."

I'm rolling off the earth. The sky crashes into the water.

I watch a young man and a little baby play in the sand. The baby's head seems too large for its body or it may be it's the mescaline which feels like acid. The mother and father and the baby look gentle. The father pats sand into a Dixie cup to make a cake for the baby. I love them all, desperately.

"What a cute baby," I say. "How old is he?"

The mother says, "Four."

Four months? Four years? I'm not sure. I don't know what babies look like anymore. I smile and go back to Ben where I belong.

He is watching a woman standing at the edge of the water. She is wearing a white bikini. The material clings to her skin like wet tissue paper. Her skin is the color of coffee. She has long black hair that looks like birds live in it. Except for her breasts she is as lean and muscular as a young boy.

"I wish you looked like her," Ben says. "A flat stomach is really sexy on a chick."

I look down at my stomach. "Some men like a gentle slope below a woman's waist."

"Well, I don't."

I want to kick in his face. I want to say, "I'm late to

meet Dennis Hopper. By the way, he says you'll never make it." I want to hitch up the Canyon in a white bikini.

I am still high. I lie in the hammock at Ben's and watch the clouds move across the sky. Ben climbs into the hammock on top of me.

"Sex is great on mesc," he says.

I don't care about sex. I just want Ben to let me stay. His body weighs down the hammock. I feel the tall grass brush against my back. The hammock swings slowly, heavily. The blue sky bleeds into the purples of the Canyon. Ben is lying on top of me. His thick hair in the curve of my neck smells like almonds. I want to stay like this forever: my body pinned down but my head free.

"Hey, Ben!" someone calls from the road.

"Come on down!" Ben calls back.

"No," I say. "I'm naked."

Ben jumps up from the hammock, pulls on his jeans. "Doesn't matter," he says. "There are always naked chicks around here."

It's taking too long to come down. I sit in Ben's straw chair that hangs like a cage from the rafter on the porch. I hug my arms close to my body and smoke Marlboros one after another. The sun is setting red on the Canyon. The Canyon turns metallic red. But I'm tired of it all, and I want it to be over.

Ben paces up and down the porch, his head down, his Stetson forward on his brow. The floorboards in the porch creak.

He stops in front of me with his back to me. He looks at the sunset. "I want a real relationship," he says.

I hug my arms closer to my body.

"I want to be in love," he says.

My eyes itch. I stare at my knees and let my eyes close.

I don't look up at Ben. I didn't come to L.A. for something real. Enough was real where I came from. I'm coming down fast now. My head drops to my knees. I suppose I have to say something to Ben. I can say I love him, that might work, but I don't love him, and, besides, I wouldn't know what to do next. My forehead is heavy on my knees.

I hear the engine and the crunch of gravel under the tires of the Lotus as Ben pulls out of the driveway.

I never do get to the macrobiotic restaurant Warren Beatty goes to.

Ashes

*Look not thou upon the wine
when it is red, when it giveth his
colour in the cup, when it moveth
itself aright.*
*At the last it biteth like a serpent
and stingeth like an adder.*
    —Proverbs 23:31–32

My mother died. She was fifty years old. She had so many times told me how she would choose to die: as her own grandmother had died, at the age of ninety, in her sleep, after digging the whole day in her own garden.

My mother did not have a garden.

When I was a child our family spent the winters in St. Petersburg Beach, Florida. On shop signs and beach towels, everywhere, there was a fat, smiling sun radiating blazing rays. On days when there was no sun at all, the newspaper was given away free. We could take the sun that much for granted.

Five months before my mother died she returned to

St. Petersburg Beach, to the Gulf Winds Apartments, as she had done each year for twenty years. One hundred miles farther south, in Miami, I lay in the sun and watched my legs turn gold. When I could not stand it anymore, I took a bus to St. Petersburg. I stayed with my mother there for one week. It was the beginning of March, and the air was cold and raw. We waited for the weather to turn.

I awake in the bed across the room from the bed where my mother has been sleeping. On her bed, the bedspread, tan with giant green palm fronds, has already been pulled over the sheets and pillow. My mother is sitting at the table by the window that looks out into a courtyard. Outside, the day is gray. There is no sun.

My mother's head bends over the table. From the back, her neck is thin, too soft and white where the spine supports the neck. From the back, too, her dark hair is thin and limp. Next to her on the table there is a coffee cup. My mother's fingers hold the cup. As another mother might carry a baby, my mother carries the cup everywhere with her. When it is empty she goes back to the cabinet underneath the sink. In the mornings she fills it with red wine; in the afternoons, with bourbon.

I sit up in bed, taking it all in: this small panorama. Each morning I have been here it has stunned me that it is still here: this room, not redecorated since the fifties, my mother in it, sitting at the window, looking out into the gray courtyard.

I stretch in bed and look at my long tan legs spread out from a short nightgown. I am twenty-four years old.

My mother turns to me. "Would you like some orange juice, Pumpkin?"

I wish she were not so nice to me. It is a superb performance, considering, but it distracts. It assumes that I am a daughter visiting my mother in Florida. It assumes my presence is not a mission or a bludgeoning—but a visit. We go to seafood restaurants and eat shrimp.

My mother does the driving; I let her. She squints through the windshield, her two hands clutching the wheel. She doesn't drive over twenty miles an hour. If she crashes I will not be hurt.

I swing my legs over the bed in slow motion. When I am up I touch my toes twenty times. I do this every morning.

My mother gets up from the table and walks the few steps to the kitchenette. She walks on brittle bones, carefully, as though each step may not carry her inches farther along the carpet but instead plunge her into an abyss that wavers at the edge of each step.

She takes a quart of orange juice from the refrigerator and pours some into the glass. I let her do these old things for me.

"Here," she says. She is smiling, but the smile hurts her. The hurt lies dark behind her eyes, betraying her smile. She doesn't see me. Her eyes howl.

I take the glass of orange juice. I try not to touch her hand.

Today is an important day. My mother and I are going to the beauty parlor. My long hair troubles her: it has always been this way with us. "I'll have it cut," I have told her, "if you will go with me and have yours done, too." And she has agreed. If she can do this one thing, perhaps she can do another harder thing, and another. My hair will grow back. It doesn't work that way with mothers.

My mother is already dressed in her soft knit bermuda shorts, a soft knit shell, and tennis shoes. She always wears tennis shoes. She polishes them with white shoe polish so that they always look clean. She has bought the same shorts and the same shells in several different colors, all pastels. Except for the change in hue—pink, green, blue—she wears the same thing every day. When she goes out of the apartment she puts on round flat earrings that look like after-dinner mints.

I sit down at the table across from my mother. I stare into the courtyard. It is windy; the umbrella cannot be raised at the round table. It hangs faded and limp on its pole. In a snapshot of my mother and me, the green and white umbrella bursts against the blue sky. My mother, in a halter and shorts, is serving me a cupcake with a lighted candle on it. She turns back to the camera, her fabulous legs and her smile daring the camera not to record her. I am five or six years old. I am wearing a pinafore and have two bows in my hair, one on either side of a center part. I smile only in the corners of my mouth.

My mother sits and smokes L&M Filters. They burn with a brown, stale smell. She smokes one after another. The movement of her hand and arm is slow, unconscious, as though the cigarette is part of her. She sips from the cup as though the cup is part of her. My mother and the smoking and the sipping in a fluid, recurring movement.

On the table there is an envelope. On it I recognize my mother's scrawl. It is familiar, but it has changed. It is light and wavy as though it had been written by someone with a pencil between his teeth. The words she has written are:

Let me live in a house
by the side of the road
And be a friend of man

"What's this?" I ask her.

She cocks her head. "Oh, it's a poem." She sounds coy.

"A poem?" It is as though my mother had appeared wearing high-heeled Carmen Miranda sandals instead of her low, white, soft-soled shoes.

"Yes." She is arch, defiant. Her eyes blaze, then go swampy. She fingers the edge of the envelope. "I can't remember it all. Just this much. I used to know the whole thing." Her eyelids sink. "This poem is what I wanted my life to be like." Her voice has become a whine. "I can't remember the rest."

I didn't know my mother ever wanted anything. Except for the usual, except what she got.

"We could go to the library," I say. "We could find the book of poetry. You could read the whole poem again." My voice sounds strange to me. "I could look it up for you in the card catalogue." My voice does not sound right anymore. It sounds like a Christmas ball breaking.

In the courtyard a white-haired woman is dragging a

chaise into a corner of the U where there is shelter from the wind coming off the Gulf. She lies down on the chaise, covers her legs with a beach towel, and raises her face as if to the sun.

I go to the bathroom to brush my teeth. There is no one in the mirror. There is my long, straight hair, my tanned shoulders, my flowered nightgown, its lavender trim soft and gorgeous against my gold skin. But the sun has bleached my hair and burned my face to the same dark ochre. My features are gone. My brow, nose, mouth are rubbed down like the features of a face on a penny that has passed through many hands.

I have just come into the bathroom, where my mother cannot see me and I cannot see her.

"Oh, Pumpkin," she calls from the other room. I stop my hand as it squeezes toothpaste onto the brush. My fingers pinch in the sides of the tube. I hold the tube above my brush, poised, and wait for her to say it. With my whole body still, I dare her not to say it. "I feel a little punky today," she says. "I don't feel like going to the beauty parlor. You go on ahead without me."

I come out of the bathroom and face my mother. The toothbrush and toothpaste are still in my hands. "You have to go with me," I say. I mean to scream the words at her, but they come out muffled and float somewhere in the space between us. I look at my mother. She is huddled into a corner of the room. She doesn't move. Her eyes howl, flash: *Please leave me alone to die. Please, I don't ask you for much.*

So this is it, then, This is what happens to people. "I won't go alone," I say.

My mother is silent and unmoving.

"I was only going so that you would go." *You are my mother and you must not die like this. You owe me that much.*

My mother is silent and unmoving. She huddles in the corner of her small room, clutching her death in her fist.

"I'll cancel our appointment," I say. I sound like a secretary.

Her eyes soften to a sob.

I phone the beauty parlor. I do it in full sight of my mother. A woman's voice answers. Her voice is warm. "May I make another appointment for you and your mother?" she asks. The way she says the words makes it sound as if it happens all the time: mothers and daughters coming to the beauty parlor together to have their hair done. She makes it sound as if it's not unusual at all.

I look across the room at my mother. She is looking down at the floor. She has grown so dark and thin here in her pastel clothes, in her Florida room. A dark thin string with brittle bones and face awash. Her eyes are half-closed.

I am four or five years old. I have awakened late at night. I run down the stairs to the toilet. As I reach the bottom stair and round the banister, I feel the pee run hot down my legs. It makes a pool on the shiny floor. It was dark and nighttime in the room where I was sleeping, but the stairs and hallway are bright as day. I blink back my hot, wet shame.

Suddenly I feel my mother standing tall above me. When I look up I see she is very tall and beautiful with a clear brow and soft dark eyes. "It doesn't matter, Pumpkin," she says. "It doesn't matter at all." Her eyes are sad, but her mouth is smiling.

My mother's head droops onto her breast. I can't see her face. I can only see the top of her head where her thin, dark hair is combed away from the part.

"Will we see you and your mother another time?" the woman on the telephone asks me.

"No," I say. "No."

Two

The Baby in Mid-Air

As she sees the baby in mid-air, her brown head falling toward the floor, her legs and red shoes above it, the mother—too far out of reach to catch her or even to break the impact of her fall—feels the moment at the base of her womb, its sides contracting with a sharp pain as though the child were being born again. There is a light thud as the small body hits the floor. There is a cry, a deepening in the color of the baby's face from ivory to red, the baby's placid face scrunched into a tight mask. The mother scoops up the baby as though she is weightless, presses her to her breast, presses her small shaking body into her own where it had once been safe, yet unborn.

The baby dances on tables. She cries out in a deep lusty voice that is unchildlike. She howls in delight at the sound her soles make on the tabletop, at her great height, at her power to yell and dance at the top of the world. The mother holds her breath as the child dances, fearing the fall from this bravado of innocence. (She imagines her own birth, emerging from her mother's womb, cautious, scanning the faces around her before she lets out her first cry.)

While she was pregnant she dreamed she left the baby

sleeping in a bar, on the seat of a booth like a pocket-book.

She dreamed she gave birth to a baby who looked like a flipper, and she embraced it, not anyway, but on its own terms.

She was told not to expect much: that her newborn child would look like a veal roast.

Her belly grew larger and she felt inside it little kicks like tap dancing, and, later, somersaults as though she housed some sort of circus or zoo. Still, she didn't believe it was a baby who caused the movement. She dreamed she sat in the delivery room, on top of the cold steel table, and while she waited to give birth, watched her belly become smaller, then smaller and smaller until it was flat. The intern, in the voice of a department store salesman, explained, "There must have been some mistake."

In the delivery room she struggles to keep her eyes open against their impulse to close as she pushes down. She must see the baby as it emerges, before it becomes air in the doctor's gloved hands.
     The baby doesn't wait to be slapped, but cries at once. The baby is complete: the mother will have to do nothing more, nothing. Already, without her knowledge or planning, there are eyes, and hands and feet with toes like pebbles, black wet strands of hair against the scalp.

The sky has darkened outside the hospital window. The baby is two hours old. The mother wakes from a

Demerol sleep, holds onto the edge of the bed as she lowers herself, tests the cold tile floor with her bare feet. She walks out into the hallway and follows the distant wail to the nursery. But a white curtain has been pulled across the nursery window. (Three years later the baby flies down the sidewalk on a red motorcycle, professionally dragging one tiny foot as she disappears around a corner.)

The nurse wheels the baby into the mother's room in a colorless, transparent plexiglass tray, closer and closer to the mother, who sees the white of the nurse's uniform, the gleaming cold white tile floor—the baby in mid-air, the white tiles, red blood spreading out around the tiny body like ripples in a pond, the nurse holding the baby out to her like an offering, the tiles, the red blood whelming over the body, a squashed fruit.

"Don't leave me!" the mother cries.

The baby is a neat, tightly-wrapped bundle in a white blanket, like a small mummy; only her face is not wrapped. Her face is a small moon, a pale light in the mother's arms, in the darkening room. The mother holds the baby lightly, like a girl carrying a bough of flowering branches across her arms.

The baby's face is calm, her eyes open, waiting for the discovery. (It is the same look the baby will have two years later when she hides by turning her back to her mother and being still.) And the mother begins to cry because the baby is not a stranger to her and her feeling for her is overwhelming and unmistakable, is what she had imagined falling in love might be like. As she looks at her child, the names she'd considered—Vanessa, Zoe,

Claire—shift in her mind, boy or girl shifts in her mind, distinctions that no longer matter.

Peripherally, she notices the flowers that arrive in high waxed paper wrapping like a bishop's hat. She sees her baby's face in the opening roses, hears her cry when the room is still. At night she lies awake and, in the light from the streetlamps, looks at the face of her watch. At six in the morning the baby will be brought to her to be fed. Her breasts burn and throb, leaking milk into small pools on the sheets.

She sees the faces of her husband and friends as though underwater; she hears their voices as echoes from a deep tunnel.

The baby in mid-air falling

She dreamed she left the baby in a booth

At home, the baby sleeps small in the vast expanse of crib, her head a small moon on the sheet. The mother lies awake, listening: a pause in the rhythm of breath, as a yawn or cough is forming, and the mother stops breathing, suspended midair until the rhythm begins again.

In the daytime, when the baby is sleeping, the mother peeks over the edge of the crib, waiting until she sees the baby's lips flutter ever so slightly as breath passes. Doing the dishes, she hears the baby's cry in the whine of the hot-water faucet; outside, she hears the baby's cry as a bus rounds the corner. The cries bleed into the quiet, and the mother lives within the cry.

The baby in mid-air

The baby is two-and-a-half, still small, with delicate bones like her mother's. She stands alone outside a barbed-wire fence, her hands cupped on either side of her mouth. She is calling the horses. "Pu-oy!" she calls her favorite horse, Pie, in her Brooklyn accent, and the horse, grazing out in the field, turns. "Hor-ses!" The baby's deep alto lifts a note on the second syllable, holds onto the "s" in an echo of the voice of the stablehand. The horses thunder toward her, stop short at the fence, and snort. The baby stands with her hands clasped behind her back, rocks back on her heels, and grins.

The mother, who is afraid of horses, shivers around the corner of the barn.

The baby in mid-air

The sturdy baby, in red boots, talks to the horses, a spirited gibberish with emphasis on the word "hay." The mother turns and walks from the barn toward the house, conscious of each foot as it passes the other, hears the neighs and the stomping and the baby's throaty squeals, and she feels a coolness on the palms of her hands like raindrops.

Snow

It's been snowing for thirty hours. The cat is restless. She whines to go out. A four-foot drift blocks the back door. She leaps to the windowsill, her body splayed across the pane like a flag. Her claws paw the glass.

I am a city person. I don't trust weather. The little match girl went to sleep in the warm warm snow. My great-grandmother rode home in horse and carriage through a blizzard. The baby on her lap suffocated in so many blankets. It was somewhere in Ontario.

The eleven o'clock news says electricity is out in Boston. Fuel supplies could be cut off to the cities. We don't have a fireplace. "Should I buy an electric blanket?" I ask my husband.

"What for?" he says.

The child is restless. She whines for candy. She takes a licorice disc that looks like a 45. She unravels it to its center and tries to use it as a jump rope. It isn't long enough. So she eats it. She comes to me with a scared, pale face. I carry her into the bathroom, feel the warm liquid seep through her pants into my shirt. I kneel on the bathroom floor, working the pants down her legs, trying to get them off without getting diarrhea on her socks. I hear footsteps on the stairs. My husband is home.

"It's a Vinter Vonderland," he booms in his fake German accent. "It's beautiful. It's quiet. It's clean. It's peaceful. The market closed at two. No trouble with the trains at all. I got right on a train as soon as I got into the station."

I come out from the bathroom with my daughter's soggy underpants. "When is the last time you saw me when I wasn't elbow-deep in shit?"

He turns to me. "Is that the kind of question you greet me with when I come home from work?"

"We live in asylums," my friend Richard, an ex-lover, tells me on the phone.

My daughter is standing on her high chair mixing potato peels with water and pepper. "I make cookies," she says.

"But you?" I ask Richard. "I was thinking about you. If I were single and living in the city, I'd go down to a bar or café, have a glass of sherry, talk to people—"

"I did that."

"You did? And it wasn't fun?"

"No."

"Why not?"

"Because the people who sit around West Side bars during the day are idiots."

"I don't believe you."

"It's true. What was that?"

The baby has fallen from her high chair into the cat litter box. She has broken the cat litter box, and the light brown litter spills out onto the floor.

"Oh, well, you had better go to her then," Richard says. "Right away."

The baby climbs onto the kitchen counter to get another licorice.

"No, you can't have licorice," I say. "It gives you diarrhea."

"I want licorice."

"You can't have licorice," her father says. "Look, I'm going out now, and when I come back I'll bring you some other candy." He opens his eyes wide and smiles. "I'll bring you a Kit Kat."

"I don't want Kit Kat. I want Kit Tac."

"Oh, you want Tic Tacs?"

"I want a Kit Tac!" She screams emphasis on the last syllable.

Her father looks at me. "Does she want a Kit Kat or Tic Tacs?"

The baby is upstairs with Carrie, who has a child the same age. I hear the two of them running across the ceiling. I sit at the window and watch the snow. I want to see that it is beautiful. The phone rings.

"Hi, it's Emmie Lou Taylor from the babysitting pool? I'm so far behind, I apologize, but I need to know how many hours you sat last month."

I go back to the window and look at the snow. It looks the same. The phone rings again.

"Hi, this is Emmie Lou Taylor. I may have just called you a few minutes ago, I'm sorry, but I lost the slip of paper where I was keeping track—"

I take the phone off the hook. A man's voice comes

on. I jump. He tells me to put the phone back on the
hook. I bury it under two pillows. The muffled voice
repeats itself over and over.

I'm in the laundry room putting the baby's pants in
the wash. I hear my husband talking to the baby in the
kitchen, but I can't hear what he's saying. I come into
the kitchen and he glares at me. He's still in his parka,
his face raw from the cold. "Answer me!" he says.

"What did you ask me?"

"I asked you if you could hear me."

"Well, I couldn't. I thought you were talking to the
baby."

"I expect an answer when I ask a question."

"When the question is 'Can you hear me?' if you don't
get an answer, you assume the person can't hear you."

He goes out again, slams the door in the middle of
my sentence.

The baby is playing with Carrie's son. The baby has a
plastic motorcycle, a Big Wheel, and a tricycle. Both
children want to ride the plastic motorcycle. My joints
are stiff, my throat hurts, and when I stand up my ova-
ries hurt. "Do you want to watch me take my temperature?" I ask the kids.

Their faces look up. They know what a temperature
is. I hope I have a temperature.

It's 98.6.

"I'm not sick," I tell them, mock-cheerful. I wonder if
my tone fools them.

I put my daughter to bed. She gets up and lies down

on the windowsill of a low window in her room. Through the insulation of the storm windows, the pane is cold.

"I sleep here," she says.

"No, you can't sleep there. It's not your bed. Lie down and put your head on the pillow." My voice is thin. It lacks resonance.

"I go to sleep here!" My daughter's voice is full-bodied. I hate her for it.

I throw her down on her bed. "Go to sleep!" I scream. My husband is in the living room, lying on the couch, reading the *Times*. He doesn't say anything. I lie down on my back on our bed and close my eyes.

"Are you going to sleep?" he calls in from the living room, accusing me.

"I don't know."

The phone rings. It's for my husband. I call him. He sits down on the side of the bed away from the phone. He pulls the cord across my body. When he's done, he hands me the receiver to hang up.

I dream I am sitting on the floor in a basement in my house. The floor has broken through to the subbasement where a large brown dog is roaming among the stones and bricks and pieces of broken cement. I have a notebook on my lap. It's quiet. I am aware that the dog is beneath me. The dog can't get to me. He is too far below. But there are other beasts, smaller ones, so small I can't see them. They have already climbed up to the basement where I'm sitting. They're there now among the debris.

I wake up when my husband comes into the room. I reach for the thermometer to take my temperature. My husband goes into the living room and lies down on the couch. He calls out to me, "I'm sleeping in here tonight."

My husband is big and warm. "Sleep in here," I say.

"No fucking, no sleeping."

"What if I had cancer?"

"Try me when you have cancer."

My temperature is 99. By morning it may rise to 100, 101, 102.

Outside the bedroom window, snow falls straight down in a continuous white drape. I draw my knees up to my chest, slip my icy hands between my thighs. I lie on the cold sheets, eyes open in the dark, and wait for the fever.

Mother's Day

I'm afraid to walk the dog alone at night, so I ask my husband to watch me from the window. I go out into the street with the dog and look up at our parlor window. It's dark there; it doesn't look like anyone is home. I yell to my husband from the street. Not as loud as I would yell if I were being attacked, but loud. There is no answer. No one comes to the window.

In the Village, on the same street where I lived, a girl was murdered. The stabs took less than ten seconds. From the description in the paper, the girl looked just like me. I wish there had been a picture so I could be certain it was not me.

I go back into the house with the dog on the leash. I call to my husband. I walk through the parlor, through the bedroom, and into my husband who is coming out of the bathroom.

"Where were you?" I ask him. "I called out."

"I had to take a leak."

"But you promised you'd watch me."

"I was watching you. I just—"

"I could have been murdered ten times while you were in the bathroom."

I go back into the street with the dog. I walk the dog

in circles in front of the house. Every time I turn, he tugs at the leash. He wants to walk forward in a straight line. I walk him around in circles in front of the house. Above me, filling the parlor window, is my husband watching over me.

It is noon on Hudson Street. The girl is walking downtown. She is carrying a small brown bag from the deli. She has a quart of Tropicana orange juice and a package of four English muffins. She is wearing a loose-fitting turtle-neck sweater and corduroy jeans. Her long brown hair has not been combed yet today.

She passes some men who are stripping antique furniture on the sidewalk. She says hi. They nod and keep on working.

She is thinking about how good the muffin will taste with sweet butter and honey on it, how good the cold juice will feel down her throat. She presses the paper bag to her breast. She can feel the cold juice carton through her sweater. Her head is down. Her fingers grope in her purse for her key. Before she can look up to see the face of the man who will fix the rest of her life at this moment in time, she feels her legs turn to butter and a cold-hot stream down her spine. She follows her paper bag to the floor. She sees the smiling orange face of Tropic-Ana peek out from the bag, and then it is dark.

It's Mother's Day. The celebration is at the Country Club. It has been an hour, and the waiter has not yet brought the salad. The children have eaten all the rolls.

Large beige crumbs litter the tablecloth. My three-year-old daughter sits in her cousin's lap while her cousin puts nail polish on her small fingernails.

My husband's cousin leans across my husband toward me. His head is cocked, his eyes narrowed, his mouth lazy. "How's Charlie treat you, hmmmn?"

It is an odd question, but I consider it. I try to answer as truthfully as I can. "Well," I say, "Charlie has quite a temper. He is very demanding—"

"What!" my husband says. "I'm not demanding at all. I make no demands on you." He leans close to me and whispers, "Tell him you don't get enough. That's what he wants to hear."

"I can't," I say.

"Why not?"

"Because I'm not a talking dog."

My best friend goes into her apartment building on Sheridan Square. She waves to the hairdresser on the ground floor whose door is open. Her slingbacks make a click clack on the stairs in the hall. In her head she is composing a tune with the click clack as backup rhythm. At her landing she puts her key into the lock of her door. She feels something cold at her temple. Inside her apartment he lays the gun and knife on her pillow. Like a director he tells her what to do. He will cut her face, he tells her, if she doesn't. So she does. But she gags on it. Ever since she was a child she has vomited too easily. She gags, but keeps her stomach muscles tight and breathes hard in and out, in and out, so she won't throw up. She isn't really *that* frightened, she tells me later, because even though he had a gun with a silencer and a knife, his face was kind.

My husband's ten-year-old daughter is drinking his vodka gimlet. Her face is yellow.

"I want chocolate milk," my daughter says.

"Here," her cousin says. She shoves towards her a cocktail glass with a pink bubbly liquid and a cherry and a thin striped cellophane cocktail straw. "Try this. It's a Shirley Temple."

"I don't want Temple," my daughter says. "I want chocolate milk."

"She doesn't know who Shirley Temple is," I say. She knows who Spiderman is. She knows the Hulk.

The waiter's collar is too tight. Above it his neck and face are raw red. "When you get a chance," I say, "please bring my daughter some chocolate milk."

He looks at me. His eyes pinch. There is panic in his voice. "I'll have to mix it myself," he says.

"Yes," I say tentatively.

"I don't know if we have chocolate syrup. If we don't have syrup, I can't make it."

"Yes. If you don't have syrup, you can't make it. Then bring her plain milk."

I push open the door to my apartment and feel his chest up against my back and his arm alongside my breast. "Goodnight," I say. I am polite. I slam the door, but its momentum is stopped. It doesn't reach the doorjamb. The lock doesn't click. The door makes a muffled thud against his body which stands halfway inside, between the door and the frame.

Inside he talks fast, and his words are disconnected. His eyes fly. He says some white women don't like black men and that makes him mad. I say, "Oh really? How awful! Oh really? Oh really?" I want to keep him talking. He comes close and I step away; he comes close and I step away. My stomach hurts. I am constipated. I was looking for a drugstore when he fell into step beside me in the empty street on the dark, rainy night. The skin on my belly is stretched too thin. My skirt hurts. If he touches me I will implode. I offer him cheese and juice. He shoves me on the bed and spreads himself on top of me. His mouth clamps onto mine, his face pressed so deep into mine I cannot breathe. I jerk my head back and forth like a gagged woman.

We are driving on the L.I.E. to the Five Towns for Mother's Day. The rain is heavy. The traffic is heavy. My husband's two daughters and our daughter are in the backseat.

My husband drives in the far right and far left lanes where the potholes are lakes. Great sheets of water slice up from the tires, slam onto the windshield. The windshield is water. I clutch the strap on my seatbelt that cuts across my chest. I work my foot from the ankle, flexing when I want my husband to brake the car. He brakes several seconds after I would have.

"Is my driving making you nervous?" he asks.

"Well—" I say.

"Christ. My ex-wife was just like you. My driving made

her nervous, too. So what did I go through all this for—
the same old thing?"

"Does that mean it's the same thing?" I inhale, but my
breath snags somewhere in my throat.

"It's just like my shrink said. We marry the same people.
When I picked up the kids, my ex-wife said, 'I'm worried
about you driving in this weather with the kids.'"

"Why do you assume that because your driving makes
your wives nervous it means your wives are nervous?
Maybe it means your driving makes people nervous."

He turns his head to the backseat. "What about you,"
he asks his ten-year-old daughter. "Does my driving make
you nervous?"

"Children have no sense of mortality," I say.

His daughter's voice is matter-of-fact. "No, your driving doesn't make me nervous. I happen to think you're
a terrible driver—"

"You what?"

"I said I happen to think you're a terrible driver, but
your driving doesn't make me nervous."

The dark street is empty. The baby has not been inside
me for six weeks; tonight the baby is not riding in its
pouch on my breast. Still, I am heavy and dark as the
night. But for a moment I feel a glimmer, a flash, of
light, of lightness: that one day my body will be my own
again.

Behind my left shoulder there is a pungent smell; it is
human; there is warm breath on my cheek. I hear words,
muffled beyond meaning, and turn to see a dark face
with ski cap pulled down to eyelids. He steps in front of
me and blocks my path, pounces like a big puppy, and

knocks me down to the sidewalk. I lie on my back on the sidewalk. His face is too dark and too close. I cannot see it. "Take my purse," I say.

"I don't want your purse. I just want to kiss you."

His lips are soft, unformed.

There are headlights on the street. He leaps up. I scream, "Help!" I am standing. The car passes. Then the light is gone.

I am lying on the sidewalk and he is on top of me. In my ears my screams sound like his hand is over my mouth, though it is not. "If you don't scream, I won't hurt you," he says. His voice is soft, his hand is light on my thigh, and it is of the end that I am frightened, when it has not been enough, and he takes my head between his hands and smashes it against the sidewalk as if he were cracking open a coconut to get to the sweet milk.

My husband's aunt calls to me across the table, "Your daughter looks just like you."

"Yes," my mother-in-law says, "she is the image of her mother. I have never seen a child look so much like her mother."

My daughter's hair gleams red-gold in the light. I'm grateful that I washed it this morning. Her plaid, smocked dress is perfect. My daughter had not wanted to wear it. "But you look so pretty," I said. "Don't you want to look pretty?" I said, as if she weren't enough without the dress.

The women at the table beam at the perfect child and at me.

Inside me, waves crash as against groins built into the sea that split the ocean's energy in two. I am concerned with the barest survival, completing this day alive. The piqué trim at the collar of my daughter's dark plaid dress is brilliantly white and stiff against her small neck.

The waiter brings a bottle of wine to the table.

My husband's brother, who is divorced, gives the toast. "To the mothers!"

"And to the fathers," says my husband's cousin, who is also divorced, "without whom there would be no mothers."

"To the waiter," I say, but no one hears me.

"To the waiter," my husband says, and everyone laughs. The waiter's hand shakes, splashing wine into glasses.

My daughter crooks her index finger at me. "Come here," she says. "I wanna tell you a secret."

I lean close to her. Her smell is soft and young and unbearable. Her voice is not a whisper but a breath. "I can't hear you," I tell her.

She puts her mouth right up to my ear. I still can't hear her. Her face implores, is deadly serious. "You have to whisper a secret just a little bit louder," I say. Her face clouds in conflict: if she whispers it soft I cannot hear; if she whispers it loud everyone will hear, and it will not be a secret.

She raises her voice only barely. I shut out everything so that I might hear her.

"Bubble gum," she whispers. "Pink."

"Pink bubble gum?" I whisper back.

"Yes."

On the road the flat heads of the streetlights give off a light that is too yellow. Within the beams the wind-slashed rain is illuminated, then lost in darkness. In the backseat, my husband's daughters are asleep with their heads on their sweaters. My daughter is lying on the backseat floor. Silently, she passes wrappers from bite-sized Nestle Crackles and Hershey's kisses. I crumple the wrappers and put them on the dashboard.

The road runs along the airport. The small lights on the runways blur in the rain. A plane wafts over the car, a huge dark shadow, then clears the high metal fence to land. The rain falls in one thick curtain across the windshield. There is a glimmer of wet red at an intersection. A truck heaves to a stop; my husband brakes. The brakes squish. The car slides to the right and to the left and stops. The rear of the truck is higher and wider than our windshield. We can see nothing but close gray metal.

"I didn't even see him," my husband says. He is stunned that with no forewarning something so big could stop him. His face is pale and strained. He is driving more carefully now. "It's crazy the way people drive, isn't it?" he says. "Look at all the cars that are passing me. They're driving too fast for conditions, aren't they?"

"They're stupid," I say. "People are stupid."

As far as I can see, there are cars filled with sleeping children, cars driven too fast by men, their wives silent beside them. The rain and the dark have dissolved the line between land and sky, and the streetlights and the headlights mingle with stars in one vast blackness.

My husband is driving slowly now. I want to pull off the road and wait for the rain and the night to be over. But there is no safe place, so this is enough. I will take my chances. I put my hand on my husband's knee. He pats my hand.

Memoir, Cut Short

My ex-husband always had blondes who did everything for him. I was a brunette who didn't like to do anything for anybody. Even after he'd found a blonde heiress who grew tomatoes in a window box because he hated the yellowish ones in the supermarket, and who knitted him a thick woolen stocking cap because he shivered whenever the temperature dropped below 70, it was our understanding that she and the rest of the blondes were inferior to me. That's what he told me and I pretended to believe him and to agree with him.

I dyed my hair blonde anyway. He told me, "You will always be a brunette. The light hair only points out more sharply how dark you are." He meant my nature. He was right. My blonde hair was a false advertisement; it promised lightness, an easiness in physical affairs, an undiscriminating generosity. I had none of those qualities, although I sometimes pretended to have all of them. I suspect I wouldn't have fooled anyone for long, though I fooled my present husband the longest; he still refers to my blonde hair with nostalgia, as it was in our earlier days before the roots grew in black.

The blonde my ex had right before me was an Alabama Baptist preacher's daughter whose little bottle of

Jergen's lotion sat above his kitchen sink. I had to throw it out along with a cupboard full of Dixie Pies, a round marshmallow and chocolate sandwich that she would have made his mainstay. It would be irrelevant if I hadn't loved him so much.

"That's her," he sneered, pointing her out to me in a restaurant. But his disparaging tone didn't fool me; he meant her to be a warning. Hair piled high in a golden beehive, a push-up bra underneath her sweater, she resembled a Playboy bunny—if that's the type you like, and I've never met a man who didn't, although most of them lie to you about it. "It drove me bananas when she tried to talk about philosophy," he said. "I couldn't cringe forever. I refused to let her talk except to say things like 'Pass the butter.'"

The point was: he could *talk* to me.

I wonder why he didn't.

I wonder why he married me if he didn't want to talk. He did want to screw, but he could have married the blonde for that. "I love you for your mind," he said. It was after we were married that I discovered he thought the best book ever written was *Youngblood Hawke*.

He wouldn't talk and I wouldn't screw. Like always, it's hard to say which came first.

Maybe he thought he was getting a Playboy bunny when he married me—not just the monthly choice but the Playmate of the Year, the kind who is working on her Ph.D. and they show pictures of her in the stacks in high-heeled shoes, smiling down at a book which, lying on her upended palm, would be impossible to read in such a position.

I even read *Youngblood Hawke* so we would have something to talk about, but I couldn't think of anything to say about it.

It was all of those things that rankled, but mostly it was the blondes; or so it seems to me this year. I have a theory about ex-husbands and wives who are so often talked about as prehistoric figures who have been dissected and had their species tagged: "She was a ballbreaker," that sort of thing. It makes everyone feel more comfortable, like most lies. But, even today, the thought of my ex leaves me feeling like an infant asleep in the position of a question mark. I am no less vulnerable to his blondes now than ever. (Even though I have made a perfect adjustment.) I remember them all, even the ones I never saw.

I not only saw but also spoke to the one he'd screwed on New Year's Eve, three weeks before we were married. Conspiratorially, she leaked that information to me at a party, sitting next to me on the floor in the dark, over bourbon and Kool-Aid. She mentioned it *as though I had already known*, which deprived me of ripping the hoops out of her pierced ears like they do in French movies. "Oh," I said, "well."

"I didn't think it was worth mentioning," my ex explained.

"Her ankles resemble unbaked dough," I pointed out.

"Hmmmm," he agreed. "I love your metaphors."

The blonde gave us a 6- by 10-foot painting for a wedding present (it was supposed to be nudes but looked like tables) and I hung it on the living room wall to hide the Muzak speaker which I hated but not as much as I hated her or him.

But even as I hate him now, I feel like there's a broken

diagonal line across my heart and that the two sides are pulsating toward each other but stop at that line.

He and I got spasms the first night we'd sleep together after an absence. His arm, as it lay across my breast, would jump like the line on an electrocardiogram. Then my foot would start up. "Twitching again?" one of us would smile. We liked the word "twitch." We liked the idea that we shared something weird and freakish and special. These blondes didn't twitch, I'm sure of it. (I couldn't bear it if they did.)

The New Year's Eve blonde came to visit me in the Village after my divorce. She wanted to leave her cat with me for the weekend. She was a stewardess. I wanted to see her in case the opportunity arose that I could hurt her in some way. I invited my most unpleasant friend to help me. We tried to imply that with her roommates of the same sex and their captain's beds she was hopelessly middle-class. It didn't work and I was stuck with her cat.

I didn't get another chance to hurt her, but I did get a shot at the heiress and at him and I almost finished him off—or so he said. There was something so comfortable in his suffering, it was hard to tell. But, so what? If revenge is sweet, it's like Tab or Diet Pepsi: hard to swallow, leaving a film on your gums that makes you feel like all your teeth are falling out.

I never saw the blonde heiress. She's beautiful. She has long, straight hair that glows like pale flames. In jeans and my ex's old shirt, she moves soundlessly about their apartment as she waters the tomatoes in the window box, as she takes her knitting to her lap: the muffler will be a surprise for his birthday. For months she has listened for clues that she might know exactly which colors he favors and she's knitting them, proportionately, into the muffler: two thirds blue and so on.

I refused to get out of bed on Sunday mornings to fix him pancakes and bacon. Yet it wasn't a matter of his wanting a maid (although he did). It was a matter of my being unkind.

I loved him, but anyone could have done a better job of it. He would have figured that out if I gave him the time.

So I didn't.

He never left me for a blonde. How could he? I was such better stuff. It was I who left him, on all four occasions, to my mind, in each case, just in the nick of time.

The suspense would have been too much, waiting around for her to come and take away my treasures: his index finger flying into the air to tap the salt shaker over a ripe tomato; his lean angular face fragmenting into a dance of triangles; his scatting in the shower, his phrasing always atonal.

Montauk

I t's a long drive back to the city from Montauk. I'm
sitting shotgun next to Norton, who is driving his
mother's Cadillac. My husband and my two-year-
old daughter, OD'ed on sun, are asleep in the
backseat. The Doo Wop Shop is on the radio. *Those oldies
but goodies remind me of you. The songs of the past bring back
memories of you.* Norton and I are singing along with the
oldies but goodies. We know the words of almost every
song. I grew up in the Midwest, so I don't know some
of the regional hits. I try to pick up the words from
Norton, coming in a little behind him but trying to
keep up.

Norton has one arm draped over the steering wheel,
half-driving. I'm sitting with my bare feet on the dash.
The traffic is bumper-to-bumper on the westbound L.I.E.,
the way it always is on a late Sunday afternoon in July.
If my husband were driving, he would be weaving in
and out of lanes or driving on the shoulder past the line
of traffic, then nosing his way back in when the shoulder
ran out. I would be in a hurry to get home.

But I'm not now. I like singing along with Norton. I
never listen to rock anymore. It annoys me to hear the
same songs I listened to in high school, hanging over
the radio in my mother's kitchen, mooning over some

guy or another. Now I only listen to WRVR All Jazz Radio. Jazz doesn't have words, and I like that. But because I'm not musically inclined, I can't remember the tunes without the words. I have an ex-husband who can scat, but I can't.

Oh, I wonder, wonder who ba doo oh who! Who wrote the book of love? I slap my knees on the offbeat. Norton taps on the steering wheel with his palm. Our voices are similar: weak, off-key, but determined, reaching for but never making high notes, straining but sounding like we're clearing our throats at low notes. Norton doesn't look at me. I can look at him because I know he won't look back at me. He looks handsome in his Hawaiian shirt. His knees are pink and tender with sunburn.

My husband, the one who's sleeping in the backseat, is ten years older than I am. He doesn't know the words to any rock and roll. When I used to sing along with the radio, he'd say, "How can you remember the words? I can't even hear the words." I wonder if I left something behind with Buddy Holly and the Platters and Fats Domino and Norton. It probably wasn't anything good, but I miss it just the same.

Problems, problems, problems all day long. Will my problems work out right or wrong? Norton and I sing the words in a sustained whine. I'm smiling because the song is perfect for Norton and perfect for me.

Friday night I am supposed to be driving out to Montauk for the weekend with my husband, my daughter, and some friends, but when their car pulls up and I see myself packed into the backseat of the Peugeot between my husband and my daughter in her car seat, I can't let myself be so crowded for so long. I watch my daughter's sweet, oval face framed by the back window, the triangular pane of glass between us. I wave goodbye until my arm hurts and the car rounds the corner.

In the apartment I sit on the couch and listen to nothing, and I like it.

But at 7:20 the next morning the telephone rings.

"Did I wake you?" Norton says. Four hours ago he has broken up with the woman he left his wife for, and he has been waiting since then to call me. So I ask him if he wants to drive me out to Montauk.

Norton pulls up in front of my apartment in his mother's Cadillac. He waits, slumped over, with his forehead on the steering wheel, his fingers spreading his blonde, frizzy hair out from his head. The back of his neck is pale. I want to touch it. Norton looks up, and his eyes below his wild, light hair are somber; his dark beard, tragic. He looks like a cross between an Hasidic rabbi and Harpo Marx. I want to stroke his uncombed beard, kiss his swollen eyelids. I am upset by wanting to do these things.

"Well, here we are again," Norton says in a high singsong as he pulls away from the curb. "Do you remember when you and I went to Montauk together?"

I show him where to turn off Atlantic Avenue to get onto the B.Q.E. He makes a sharp left, cutting off a Brunckhorst's delivery truck, its red lacquered side with the boar's hairy snout flashing past the window as he slams the brakes. His right arm extends stiff in front of my chest to keep me from flying into the windshield. But I'm wearing a seatbelt. He isn't.

"Whew," I say, and sink down into the seat. I'm angry

that Norton almost killed me, but I'm grateful that he tried to save me.

"That wasn't even close," he says.

"How many years ago?" I ask Norton. "You still can't drive a car. It was the same Cadillac, right?"

"Uh huh." Norton is driving in the right-hand lane of the B.Q.E. with the pickup trucks and the senior citizens. "We took your mother's dog with us. What was its name?"

"Froufrou."

"Froufrou. Does she still have it?"

"It died. It had a heart attack at the Puppy Palace. I told you that."

"I forgot. It was a nice dog. It was trained to use the toilet in your mother's apartment, wasn't it?"

Norton nods.

"I was pissed off at you that weekend."

Norton raises his hands. His shoulders take on his long-suffering slump. "So what's new?" he says.

"We had to leave the beach at two in the afternoon. You wanted to beat the traffic. I wanted to stay. We ate lobster at Gosman's, and you said to me, 'You have the most beautiful eyes I have ever seen.' The Pepperidge Farm rolls were cold. They must have been refrigerated."

"You still do," Norton says.

"What?"

"Have the most beautiful eyes. *You* know."

"Your ex-wife had beautiful eyes."

"It was makeup."

It's so early there's no traffic on the L.I.E., but I hate

the L.I.E. It slices right through the front yards of split-levels and two-family houses that all have the same fa-cade. The L.I.E. is divided by a low metal bar bent out of shape by cars crashing into it. I prefer the Southern State Parkway. It cuts through what looks like forests with the backs of suburban houses only barely visible through the trees. If you squint your eyes you can't see the houses at all. The highway dividers are of rough-hewn wood. They are intact.

We are approaching Lefrak City where you can turn off the L.I.E. and get on the Grand Central Parkway that takes you to the Southern State. If my husband were driving, he would edge the car to the right-hand side of the right lane of the L.I.E., and he would say, "Should I stay on the L.I.E.?" I would say what I always say: "No." And he would straddle the V in the highway that separates the L.I.E. from the Grand Central Park-way, turning his head to the left to see if there's traffic on the L.I.E., driving up the narrowing horizontal lines until he either had to turn to the right or to the left or drive into a strip of dried-up grass, and then he would jerk the wheel to the left and continue on the L.I.E.

I ask Norton, "Would you take the Grand Central to the Southern State? I don't know if it will get us where we're going, but it goes in the general direction."

Norton says, "Sure."

I look for a road map in the glove compartment so I can figure out where we're going from here. But there's no road map. There's a pair of sunglasses with one lens missing and a half-eaten roll of Certs.

"I never heard of a glove compartment without a map," I say.

"No one in New York uses road maps."

"How do they get any place?"

Norton shrugs. "You've got me."

"Norton, the day you and your ex-wife signed your separation agreement, she came over to my apartment. She told me you used to say to her, 'Why don't you go to the movies or something with Molly?'"

"Well, *I* didn't want to go to the movies with her."

"And she said she used to tell you, 'But I hardly know Molly, and she lives in Brooklyn, and she has a baby. She can't just drop everything and go to the movies with me.' She was wringing her hands."

Norton says, "You know when I first started going with you, it was like I had just discovered sex. It was so terrific. I mean, it was really extraordinary."

I try to remember. Images of Norton and me shuttle across my mind: Norton pressing me into the white wall of my bedroom; Norton and me sitting on the Morton Street pier in the afternoon, my sweater on Norton's lap and my hand under my sweater; Norton lying on top of me on the cool parquet floor in his apartment during our lunch hour; Norton and me wrapped around each other in some uptown movie theater while *Closely Watched Trains* plays on the screen. I never think about these things. I tend to think Norton and I have always been the way we are now.

"What happened?" I ask him.

"About two blocks before we'd get to your apartment you would start getting a headache or a stomachache or you would start to sneeze. When we got in bed, you were only interested in cuddling."

"And you started getting up in the middle of the night and bringing Sara Lee banana cake into bed with us."

"I don't remember that," Norton says.

"It's true. Your hips started to spread." I think about it for a minute. "But I mean before all that. What happened?"

We reach the end of the Southern State and stop at a gas station to pick up a road map. I like reading road maps. I am amazed that by looking at colored lines on a piece of paper you can get anywhere you want to go. If it had been left to me, there would be no road maps. I would get on one road and go into someone's house and stay there, trying to figure out what's going on. My father once said to me, "If everyone in this country were like you, there would be no roads or bridges built." He was right. On the other hand, so what?

I want to take the road that has the thinnest line on the map. When I was a girl on the way from Illinois to Florida, my mother took over the driving from my father and got on a dirt road in Georgia that led us into a cemetery. A little circle of black people stood around a grave as we passed by in our Oldsmobile.

I tell Norton, "We can get on 27 and pick up 27A near Sayville. 27A runs into 27 anyway, but if we take 27A it might be a more picturesque ride."

"I'm in no hurry," Norton says.

On 27A we are caught in a steady stream of Saturday shoppers. Traffic is bumper-to-bumper with cars turning in where it says Enter and coming out where it says Exit. In the parking lots, people are wheeling giant metal carts right up to their cars and unloading into the trunks. Whole families stand around watching.

"Maybe this wasn't such a good idea," I say.

"It's all right," Norton says.

The air-conditioned air in the Cadillac is singeing my nostrils. I push the button and the window on my side of the car goes down with a whine. I let my bare arm hang out the window in the hot, thick air. Norton doesn't put his window down, and he doesn't turn off the air conditioning.

"You know the first time you introduced me to your friends, you said, 'This is Molly. She's from Illinois. She used to be a twirler.'"

Norton laughs a high he he he he.

"It made me feel like I had six fingers or was a pin-head."

Norton doubles over. He has always found the word "pinhead" funny.

"You didn't take me seriously," I say.

"Neither did you." He's not laughing anymore, but his cheeks are still wet.

"Take you seriously? Or take myself seriously?"

"I bought you acrylic paints and canvasses. I took you more seriously than you took you seriously."

"I didn't want to paint. I wanted to get married."

Norton lets out some air between his teeth. "I was twenty-two years old. You wanted to get married and move to Westchester. You had never even been to West-chester. Anyway, I said I'd do it."

"But you were lying. You wouldn't have, would you?"

"Maybe."

We stop at the McDonald's on the outskirts of South-ampton. In high school, my girlfriends and I used to drive through the McDonald's parking lot all night look-ing for the guys who were driving through looking for

us. We always missed each other. They didn't have Big
Macs then, just small hamburgers. I feel silly standing
in line with Norton.

We take our Big Macs and sit at a stone table at the
edge of the parking lot surrounded by trash cans that
say THANK YOU.

Norton takes large, ragged bites out of his Big Mac. I
can see he is really very hungry. His hands are shaking,
and that scares me. Maybe there's more to all of this
than we're making out.

"Are you okay?" I ask him.

He nods, but I can see that he's not and that he's
grateful I asked.

"I'll drive the rest of the way," I say.

"You don't have to."

The first thing I do when I get in the car is turn off
the air conditioning and press down all the window but-
tons. The window on the driver's side and the two back
windows sink simultaneously. I press the gas pedal just
to test it, and the Cadillac lurches onto the highway. I
look over at Norton to see if he's going to say anything,
but his eyes are half closed.

Norton sleeps all the way through Amagansett. We
are on the flat open road that follows the ocean along
Napeaque Beach to Montauk. The clear, cool, salty air
blows through the car into my face. I sit up a little
straighter and shake my hair down my back. I look
over at Norton. He's awake now. I ask him if he had a
nice nap.

"I wasn't asleep," he says. "I was just resting."

We pass the motel where Norton and I stayed for the
weekend with his mother's dog. "How many years ago
was it?" I ask him.

"Seven."

"Seven?"

"You're my oldest friend."

Norton's head is erect, but his shoulders are drooping. The left side of his cheek is red and wrinkled from pressing against the leather seat back while he was asleep. We're almost to Montauk. All of a sudden I feel generous towards Norton. I want to give him something.

"I ate my first mango with you," I tell him. "We were stoned. You had this fruit that looked like a football with the air let out, and you cut me a slice. It was a carnival in my mouth. The oily taste and the sweet taste fighting each other and merging. I'll never forget it. Of course I was stoned."

Norton clears his throat. He has a look of passionate annoyance. He's staring straight ahead, not looking at me. "We're almost there," he says. "No one knows we're coming. We could turn around right now. You could just pull off the road and turn around. We could stay at one of the motels we passed, or we could drive back to the city. Anything you want."

But I'm concentrating on my driving. We're on the Old Montauk Highway now, a two-lane road that rises and falls through winding hills. The Cadillac climbs the road, its hood far in front of me, and I can't see anything ahead but the top of the hill and beyond that, sky. When I was a girl and my father was driving, I was afraid he would drive right over the edge, and I held my breath. I hold my breath now as the front of the Cadillac rises up on air where there is no more road. Then the road levels off and I can see ahead. There's no drop-off, not even a sharp curve, just more of the same road.

The Birthday Party

September 26, 1980.

It is my daughter's sixth birthday.

We are sitting in the back of Burger King, waiting for the party to begin. Our section is roped off, red crepe paper tied across the aisle, echo of pews decorated for a wedding. Each place is set with red and blue and yellow balloons sitting like giant Easter eggs inside gold Burger King crowns. My daughter has brought her own party hats, especially chosen: stand-up crowns of pink cardboard with pink confetti and silver glitter spelling out HAPPY BIRTHDAY. The price stickers are still on the backs: 49¢, Woolworth.

She is wearing one now.

A week ago she chose her party clothes—not a Cinderella dress to complement the crown, but her new Jordache jeans and Jordache sweatshirt with the logo of the wild mustang. She sits next to me, a pile of crowns and plastic bags of balloons and bubble gum and lollipops spread out on the table before her. She is silent and still, staring at the door.

I am terrified.

Parties are revealing, and I fear what I might learn this year. Last year, her fifth birthday, when I brought the cake to the dining room table and seven little girls in party dresses began singing "Happy Birthday," my daughter burst into tears. I don't know why. She would not blow out the candles on her cake. I don't know why either.

I hold my breath.

I look around Burger King, the bright yellow booths, the fluorescent lights, the hanging plants, alive and thriving in so much plastic. A birthday party in Burger King means we are refugees. Our Bowery loft, sublet from a sculptor, is no place for little girls' parties. Its walls are peeling. "It's falling apart," my daughter has said. It's not home. What was, I left and her father laid claim to. There is nothing in the co-op deed about birthday parties.

The party begins at four. Six years ago at four, I was on the delivery table, poised between pain and wonder, waiting for the birth. Aware then that there was no turning around, no choice, no opportunity to say, I take it all back, I am not ready for this, the baby would be born.

On my daughter's first birthday I served champagne and brie, strawberries and dark chocolate cake from a patisserie. My daughter pushed huge hunks of cake into her mouth, smeared icing on her dress, her face, her toys. But it was not meant to be her party. It was mine. A celebration at the end of my first year in a life with new rules where everything matters.

My daughter counts on her fingers the names of her sixteen guests: Emily, Josh, Rachel, Andrew . . .

"Andrew won't be here," I say, as though it is no cause for alarm. "We forgot to invite him."

"Invite him now," she says.

"It's too late."

How many things, great and small, have I forgotten?

"I'm a terrible mother," I said to a friend on Mother's Day.

"You're a good mother," he said. "Or else you couldn't say you're a terrible mother."

I wonder if he was right.

Because of the divorce, I watch my daughter more closely now: to assess the damage. In the mirror on the far wall we look casual enough: a mother and daughter, waiting for the birthday party to begin. I affect the same sureness I tried while a student of mine read aloud her prize-winning story at an awards ceremony. She could not have written it without me, she announced, though it wasn't so. I leaned back, arms folded, looking as if nothing could go wrong. As she read, my breath stopped with every word. And to me, for the first time, her story sounded flat and her voice shrill, her gestures were all wrong, she was trying too hard, and when it was over I breathed easily throughout the resounding applause.

The front door swings open and the first guests come in: two six-year-olds and a three-year-old brought by the neighborhood babysitter, a white-haired woman with sturdy bare legs and few teeth, pushing a sleeping baby in a stroller, the three guests holding onto the sides.

My daughter is up front at the door to greet them. She gives them each a birthday crown and a piece of bubble gum from her bag. And then another child arrives and another. She is in the swirl. I sit back and watch my daughter, so grown up in her stylish jeans, and I feel again the exhilaration I felt as I watched her being born. She is doing it all right, not out of decorum but out of feeling for her guests and the occasion, as a true hostess would. Without my having shown her, she is gracious.

How she has grown since she was two, and the clusters of balloons hanging from the kitchen ceiling made her scream and scream.

One night at the beginning of the divorce I lay on my foam slab on the concrete floor of the loft, in terror of the night, of the next day, and the day after that. I heard my daughter get out of bed, and I followed the sounds of her footsteps as she walked the full length of the loft to the bathroom and back. Her footsteps were solid, the only sound in the dark night. She had learned to walk alone, surefooted, in the dark.

Resplendent in her pink crown, standing at the front of sixteen children, my daughter leads Simon Says. When the game has ended, she gives balloons to the children whose balloons have popped. As she picks up a green balloon, it bursts in her hand, and she cries, loud, un-hampered, burying her body into mine.

"It's all right," I say. "What's wrong?"

"The noise scared me," she says.

The divorce has gone on for six months and will go on until it is over. Today my daughter received a birth-day card from her great-grandmother, my grand-mother, my mother's mother. In it, there was a note to me. Eighty-seven years old and blind in one eye, she has traveled alone on the senior-citizen bus to an eye sur-geon forty miles from her home. In her neat script, on lines made perfect by holding a ruler under her pen, she writes, *It is terrible to be alone and have to make your own decisions. Maybe I will not have that many more to make.*

I think about my grandmother now, see her sitting on the senior-citizen bus, ankles together, holding her pocketbook firm in her lap. She, fifty years older than I, her husband dead, all of her children dead, her grandchildren and great-grandchildren scattered along the coasts while she remains in a shrinking town that hugs the Mississippi, with no planes or trains, in or out.

In her orange cap and apron, smiling just as true as in a commercial, the Burger King waitress brings the cake, with requisite pink frosting and multicolored candles. The children, first haltingly and then with lust, begin to sing "Happy Birthday."

Standing at her place, hands braced on the table's edge, my daughter draws in her breath, and in one strong exhalation she blows out all her candles.

The Don

Standing alone at the end of St. Petersburg Beach, a strip of white sand that curves into the Gulf of Mexico, a mammoth Spanish structure, the Don Ce Sar Hotel, splashes unabashedly pink against the blue sky. It is a building that so captures the imagination that thirty years ago it inspired one woman from Georgia, seeing it for the first time, to return home, pack up her kids in the family Ford, and, without leaving a note for her husband, drive south to fulfill the first dream she had ever had, or at least the first one she could remember: to live within sight of the Don.

Stupid woman: to leave everything she knew in exchange for a dream of pink rising from white sand into blue sky. Stupid woman: as it happened, she turned over her life savings to an aging Florida gentleman in exchange for a house in full view of the Don, merging her dream and her reality, a house on Gulf-front property that, thirty years later, is worth $200,000.

I don't know the woman. Shortly after I moved to Florida from New York I met the woman's daughter, whose daughter was in kindergarten class with my own. She told the story briefly, in perhaps three sentences, as we waited in the Clearwater train station with the kindergarten class, all twenty-five of them swinging their legs from the benches, waiting for the train. She didn't tell the story to me. I overheard her. Which is to say that this is all I know of the woman from Georgia who has stayed with me so well. It's her dream of the Don that we have in common, and her literal-minded way of incorporating a dream into the everyday.

The woman from Georgia must have been about twenty-five when she first saw the Don. I was six. Because my dream began earlier than hers, while I was a child, it may have taken an even stronger hold, but since it was based on a childhood view, it may have been even less easy to realize.

Thirty years ago, about the time the woman from Georgia saw the Don for the second time, this time for good, arriving in St. Petersburg in the family Ford packed with the kid's clothes, the mixing bowls, a tricycle tied to the roof, and her life savings tucked into an envelope pinned to her brassiere, I saw the Don for the first time.

Imagine the sight of the Don to the eyes of a six-year-old from the landlocked Midwest! From the family's rented green-and-orange striped cabana at the north end of St. Petersburg Beach, I languished in the presence of the Don. There was no Holiday Inn then, no Hilton—bastard newcomers—only small, flat motels that in the glare of the noon sun or the haze of sunset melted, diffused, into the scrub far back from the Gulf. There was nothing to break the clean, white line of the sand strip that ran two miles from where I sat, then dipped and curved out into the Gulf, and at the end, with nothing to rival it, high above white sand and blue Gulf, rising into the sky, the massive Don.

At that time, and for many years thereafter, the Don

was no longer a great hotel, but, in a triumph of mis-matching form and function, it housed the Veteran's Administration. I mention this only for historical accu-racy. It did not intrude on the dream; it was what the Don inspired, not what it was used for, that mattered.

It is historically accurate, also, that though I was a dreamy child who had good reason to prefer fantasy to reality I was still a child. Far from the shadow of the Don, I built drip castles in the sand, and on days so cold and windy that the cabanas were left to lie folded on the empty beach, my body was thrown off a rubber raft again and again, into the choppy surf and onto the shelly coast. In other words, I did the usual things.

As winters passed I grew tired of sandcastles, tired of raking my body against the shells at surf's edge, but the dream of the Don persisted. I wish I could say it was some other dream. I wish I could say my dream was to become the architect who built the Don. Perhaps girls have dreams like that today, but they didn't in 1949. Or at least I didn't. The dream was this: at the Don, on the veranda, couples are dancing. They are all wearing white. I am wearing white chiffon. A man in a white tuxedo approaches me. He has white hair. He looks like Cesar Romero. Our eyes meet. And that's where it ended, the beginning, middle, and end absorbed into The En-counter.

Of course! It was a dream of love. My childhood vision of wafting about in white in an eternal dance was a dream of communion between man and woman. Much later, I would discard that dream and apply myself to things more mature and modern, to "working relationships" instead of love affairs. I didn't know that dreams have a tenacity of their own, not visible in their elusiveness, and that we ignore them at our own peril.

The woman from Georgia is fifty-five years old now. She sits on her patio on the Gulf. It is early morning. She sips a cup of instant coffee. She says to a friend who is visiting, "Do you know that for thirty years I have awakened to see this same sight, the light becoming bright, illuminating the white of the sand, the blues of the sky and the Gulf, and the pink of the Don, and every morning it has been as breathtaking as it was the first time?"

There was a lapse of thirty years between the first time I saw the Don and the first time I entered it, long after it had been restored to its birthright as a hotel. In those years I had done the usual things. I had married and divorced. I had learned and forgotten how to cast astrological charts. I had married again, and was divorcing again. I had had a child, a daughter.

As it happened, after thirty years, when I entered the Don I was not especially aware of where I was. I might have been anywhere, and I entered under a false identity. To the desk clerk, I gave my name as Vanessa Bell, the name of Virginia Woolf's sister. My first husband, to whom I was returning after fifteen years, paid for the room with his MasterCard. I whispered to him in the elevator: "This morning in New York, when I left my apartment for the airport, there was a man across the street squatting on a fire hydrant. He was wearing a trench coat and sunglasses. When I came outside he followed me to the corner, where I got into a taxi. The only thing that makes me think he wasn't a detective is that he looked exactly like a detective."

All the way to the seventh floor in the elevator and down the long, dark corridor to the room, I told him of lawyers, of trial dates—grade-B movie stuff, except it was real life. I was in Florida, against the advice of my lawyer, having followed instead the reasoning of another lawyer, who said that even if adultery could be proved, it would not incriminate me because it was with a man I had once been married to. I told this to him in the elevator and said, "I guess it's more acceptable as long as you keep it in the family. It would probably be even better if I were here with my father."

After thirty years of life where things didn't go exactly right or wrong, I was beginning to live the dream within the walls of its symbol. No white chiffon, but a dream of communion between man and woman. As I said, I wasn't thinking about it especially. I was thinking about the detectives.

In the room, my first husband turned on the air conditioning. I pulled back the drapes and through the white, gauzy curtains that hung behind them the Gulf burst into blueness. I sat down at the table by the window and took out of my bag the small bottle of California burgundy I had bought on the plane. I unwrapped the plastic hotel glasses and poured the wine. "What if he gets her?" I asked. "What if I have a crazy judge and a crazy jury and he gets her?"

My first husband stood behind me and put his hands on my shoulders. "He can't get her. Even mothers who are hookers and drug addicts get their kids."

"I don't think the air conditioning is working," I said. I got up and opened the window. A warm breeze blew the white curtains like scarves off to the sides of the window. Between the Gulf and the sky, a sailboat moved slowly across the horizon. My first husband stood behind me and rubbed his hands up and down my bare arms. "You're finally here," he said.

Outside, on the beach, we lay on the hot sand. I fell asleep and dreamed I was in New York, in a Brooklyn wasteland of abandoned buildings, their windows boarded up, their yards filled with old newspapers and broken bottles. The streets were maze-like and empty, and I couldn't find my way home. When I woke up, the shadow of the Don covered me, but the air was warm.

"Look up there," my first husband said.

The Don loomed above, as it had since before we were born, a dusky rose now in the setting sun.

"Look up there at our room," he said.

I followed the line where his arm was pointing until I saw the window of our room. In the massive hotel, from where we lay on the cooling sand, the windows seemed small, as the sailboat had seemed small from the window above, and in the pink grid of hundreds of windows ours was the only open window. Inside it, the curtains moved in a wafting white dance.